For Erik and Emma,
who left

First Montag Press E-Book and Paperback Original Edition June 2014

Earlier drafts of the stories *Stay* and *Man of Merritt* contained herein previously appeared in *The Masters Review* and *The Dying Goose,* respectively.

Montag Press
ISBN: 978-1-940233-08-6
Cover art © 2014 Chloé Meynier
Cover, layout, & e-book © 2014 Rick Febré
Author photo © 2014 Megan Fraudendorfer

Montag Press Team:
Project Editor – Charlie Franco
Managing Director – Charlie Franco

A Montag Press Book
www.montagpress.com
Montag Press
536 E. 8th Street
Davis CA, 95616 USA

Montag Press, the burning book with the hatchet cover, the skewed word mark and the portrayal of the long-suffering fireman mascot are trademarks of Montag Press.

Printed & Digitally Originated in the United States of America
10 9 8 7 6 5 4 3 2 1

STAY

STORIES

By Zachary Amendt

MONTAG

STAY

STORIES

By Zachary Amendt

TOWN BUSINESS

FOURTH BORE

Man of Merritt

Conversational Braille

TWO IOTA

PARALLEL FIFTHS

Barbasol Meringue

Q & A's

TOWN BUSINESS

Luther built the first scraper unicycle. He liked a dissonant jazz and his mother's bean pies. He was a Labrador, that loyal. His affinities were those of Zorro and Robin Hood: his sidekicks, Jihaad and King, were his flankers. They could fight, throw down. The *padre* at Saint John Coltrane Episcopal Church also had his back.

Luther had plans, high aim. It was only a few months away. He would graduate Skyline High as Salutatorian. He applied to universities in New York, Boston. Oakland was big, hard to police, in receivership. Three thousand miles away was his minimum. He would not look back.

His parents were Delight and Selma Bartram, uncool at times, old, but Luther was not on a leash. At 14 he asked to get a job, work nights, vend peanuts at A's games, a kiosk at Westfield Mall where he peddled tea. Sex-Ed made him interested in his lineage, but it was a soft-boiled curiosity. He didn't want facts, just names, the basics. Selma started him on *Roots*, which she kept on VHS.

It was a dramatization, she explained. It was the seventies.

Delight and Selma had put the good kind of pressure on him. High school was minuses and pluses, incentives for good marks: a new car battery, a newer used car. His acceptance into the spring pre-collegiate institute, 12½ Grade, at Columbia University put him in a different strata, but on the streets a degree from CSU Hayward was still more legit.

'Streets' implied more than one. The Bartrams lived at 2110 International Blvd., a quiet family on a promenade of subwoofers, in the only house in two square miles without bars on the windows. Luther described his neighborhood the same way Bogart had told the Nazis in *Casablanca* how there were parts of New York they were smart not to invade. Drive-bys were not uncommon, bystanders were hit – the intended target was usually the only one unscathed. The cops stopped responding. Int'l was like a speedway. The crosswalks were perilous. It was safer to accelerate than to brake.

For Luther, sneaking out after curfew was like Little League. It took practice to get good at it. It was also like shore leave: Luther and Jihaad and King didn't know the rules verbatim but they got the gist. Luther could not be peer-pressured. He had a conscientious objection to group photos, graffiti, though at times he couldn't resist making his mark on the world. He confined his tagging to the narrow grout in bathroom stalls, between the tiles. He used an erasable pen. Sharpie was too thick.

Groutcho Marx, he wrote. *Grout Ol' Opry*.

Selma was the team mom of their gang, which was unnamed until King suggested something old school and Luther proposed 'The Lyceums.' They liked that Selma sent them home with leftovers and never asked for the Tupperware back.

Selma disliked King. His bangs fell to his chin. He had to part them like a curtain call to read menus, people. He ate sloppily. He slurped. He needed more supervision, not less.

She preferred Jihaad. Jihaad thought in strikethroughs, ideas which King shot down. Jihaad had a large family. His half-siblings were half-nelsons. He evaded them. He got out of holidays. He called Selma 'ma'am' and billeted on the trundle in Luther's room whenever there was trouble at home. He modulated, unlike King, who was tempestuous, curt, and who bragged about breaking car windows without making any noise. King, who spent senior-year Civics in semi-sleep. Plagiarism was easier – simply cut and paste – until the counselors caught him.

It wasn't his fault, he said. Someone else had already said what he was thinking.

"King's a feral person," Selma told Luther. "He needs more tough-shit moments."

In her calculus, King was a delinquent. Selma wanted to reform him. There were solutions for degeneracy and vagrancy, simple ones, pills he could take.

"His heart's broken," Luther said. "Can't you tell?"

"Over a girl? Who would date him? He's not you. He's not suave."

"Not one girl. All girls," Luther said.

Her son was patient with his friends. It was remarkable. She wondered where it came from. It also baffled King and Jihaad. Luther turned down body shots. He volunteered to DD.

The Lyceums were not threatening but they lifted together at Power Alley and were built, tight-knit. They only played pick-up basketball but they could make the Skyline team easy, alley-oops. When they walked through the Quad the white girls, congregated in cliques, drew their purses closer. Stereotypes were timesavers. Some were pregnant as sophomores, others even earlier. The junior high schools had day-care units.

At lunchtime after 4th period the Lyceums convened in the cafeteria for *bro yo*: spiking their skim milks with Hennessey, a fifth of which King carried around with three lubricated condoms. It was bonding, in lieu of a bar, in lieu of El Gato Negro where they were not carded. King raised his cup. In his sunglasses he was not hiding a hangover but a black eye.

"To thug life," he said.

"Thug life?" Luther wiped off his moustache. "Your middle name is Orville."

Luther was leaving for Kennedy Airport the next day. 12 ½ Grade would eat up his Spring Break and he would miss the school dance, the Fling. When he wasn't invited to the institute at NYU, his first choice, he was Eeyore for a minute, hangdog, but fuck them, King said, it was too far from home. So was Stanford.

"I still don't get it," King said. "You already committed to Columbia, so why go?"

"It's to immerse me," Luther said.

He wanted to go where it was *at*, where it was *happening*. He knew that was New York – he had seen *Fame* a dozen times. Those were his kind of people. There were things he wanted to do which he had only read about, enviously: surf the 7 train to Citi Field. Hit on the secretaries in Varvatos pressing in at Gilt. Max out Delight's credit card at Palm Court.

"You can do all of that here," King said.

He was like a student on a dig. King had the patience for change, an excitement for shards. Oakland was a port town, not a marina town like San Francisco. The census was topsy-turvy. The ghettos were not vertical.

"Say you two. Look at this," Jihaad said, licking his thumb. "A gay character in Spiderman. Finally!"

Jihaad was also into graphic novels. King did things to him, hazed him, pants'd him at Food-4-Less, as if he was

clandestinely filming. The gossip girls, still in earshot, snick-
ered. King whistled at them. He was onomatopoeic. The
cha-ching of cash registers, flatulence.

"Which one do you like?" Jihaad asked.

"Ladasha," King said.

"The fat one?"

"That's how she spells it. La – ah."

King wrote it down. Luther wondered who came up
with these names. Viagra. Beyonce.

"She's large and in charge," Jihaad said.

"Let he who hath never fucketh a fat chick cast the first
stone," Luther said.

In the second semester of his senior year Luther
stopped chasing girls. It was tiresome. He let them come
to him. They made fun of his brains. He didn't talk street.
They were jealous of his 'fro. It didn't deter him. The last
girl he exhibited any interest in was Lyn Le, the varsity la-
crosse captain, and he asked her out not with roses but with
a bouquet of broccoli he swiped from the cafeteria. She was
ensconced in Prada, a statement garment which fell like a
trenchcoat to her ankles. They didn't always have vegetables
at lunchtime. Nachos were a daily staple.

"Let's serenade Ladasha," Jihaad told King.

"Don't."

"I can see clearly now the rain is gone," Jihaad crooned.

"Please stop."

"I can see all the popsicles in my way."

In the first semester of his senior year Luther was the
romantic, the ebony Cary Grant. He wore slacks and two-
tone shoes and put technology in air-quotes, "the internet,"
"phones." He had taken a bite out of the bouquet waiting for

Lyn to say yes. Everyone in the cafeteria stared and when she nodded they clapped and huzzahed. It was October and for a first date they snuck into the R. Kelly concert at the Paramount and drank Cognac and Cokes on fake IDs. Lyn lived in the Crocker Highlands on a cul-de-sac with twenty-foot gates and a private security guard.

Luther didn't know why she went to public school. It was like she was slumming. He wanted to introduce her to Selma.

"I invited her for dinner," he said. "Bean pies. Your best dish."

"I'd rather you didn't," Selma said.

Luther's good mood evaporated.

"You don't realize," she said. "Just as I get close to these girls you dump them."

"You were never seventeen," Luther said.

Lyn had not been the first. It turned out her coat was a knock-off. Her erudition, also, was faux. She told him she loved him after the concert, then rescinded it. It was the alcohol, she said. You got me drunk. It was just short of love. She was still fond of Luther but out of his reach. Her world was one where the man wore his napkin around his neck, instead of in his lap. He and Lyn wouldn't fit. Inevitably he would do something uncouth, wake up in the middle of the night in the kitchen on his tiptoes, urinating into the sink like Belmondo in *Breathless*. Lyn did all the preemptive work. *She* broke up with *him*. For that, she had his undying groutitude.

::

Delight had a little money which he played the markets with. He was a sucker for penny stocks and ForEx and did not always win but usually recouped the principal. Selma's world was not safe for that kind of adventure, motorcycles without helmets, staggering debt. She had the mind of a baker, precise, by-the-book. She biopsied every mole.

"You're driving Luther to the airport," Selma said.

"When?"

"Tonight," Selma said.

Delight had forgotten about 12 ½ Grade. His mind was a sieve, a colander.

Their thirty years of marriage were catalytic decades, more deaths than births, some property left behind by relatives, DUIs. It was not a boring partnership, though Delight could understand how, from the outside, it might look that way. Kaiser employed them both, Delight at the steel plant and Selma at the hospital on MacArthur. Well before Luther and years before Delight (who she met at a Bobby Searle rally, in the days when everyone got laid at political demonstrations) she sang huskily in nightclubs and groped herself during the choruses (like Billie) and made love with a series of unqualified failures: the disgraced librettists, novelists who were one-and-done. She had a way of making men feel small. It was not travel that Delight offered her, but wider travel, cruises to Anchorage and Crete in staterooms instead of steerage.

When Luther came to her – late in life, at 46 and on Christmas of all days, her Christmas miracle – she nearly ceased being. She found her first gray hair, her second. She recalled Greece in the same manner she described Caesar's Palace, and her favorite restaurants became those with early-bird specials, family-friendly joints where the chef got her the hookup. It was a near-geriatric happiness amounting to close parking spots, haggling at flea-markets, trolling the farmers' market before everything was picked through. She had front-door wreaths for every occasion, Thanksgiving, Kwanzaa. She had four backup first-aid kits.

"Remind me, what airline?" Delight asked.

"Just make sure he's got his umbrella," Selma said.

Luther played favorites. It was his only-child prerogative. Delight knew Luther preferred Selma's company. She allowed a modicum of disorder, but Delight was more laid-back than Luther thought he was, more hip. He made molehills out of serious setbacks. He drove recklessly to the airport. He sped.

They turned onto Doolittle, under the FLY OAK signage. At the United terminal he parked and shook Luther's hand. A motor officer motioned for Delight to drive on.

They hadn't said much. Delight had splurged on the ticket and bought Luther a first-class seat, money he had once spent on himself, both ways. In his middle age he did not succumb to the material things, the jet-skis or hot tubs or vinyl siding. He banked vacation time, didn't use it, cashed out. He put Luther ahead of Selma, sold timeshares to buy him a Chevy Caprice on his 16th birthday, rims. He was just as economical with discipline. He couldn't remember raising his voice. He never used the belt.

Oakland was common sense to Delight. In forty years they went from installing a Klansman as Alameda County Sheriff to nearly electing a Black Panther as Mayor. Fruitvale used to have beer gardens, a Turnverein. After the war the Germans who had settled it fled to Lafayette, the

Creek. The house on International wasn't the grey lady he and Selma wanted in Piedmont, but it was what they could afford. That was 1983. It had been safe. In the other neighborhoods Blacks were still forbidden to buy.

::

Luther's plane was delayed. He had been in New York for more than a week and unreachable, except by 'text.' Jihaad and King drove in laps around the airport, in King's Nova outfitted with nitrous and hydraulics. It was eating up gas. King lost his cool gradually. He wished life was as seamless as it was in the movies, *Jurassic Park*, *Beverly Hills Cop*. High school had not been instructive. He didn't know how to pack a bowl, or read the news. There were no silver linings in genocide, but he tried to find them regardless.

"I wish Iraq had been about oil," he said to Jihaad. "It might still be $1.50 a gallon."

It was the thing that got him shushed out of jazz clubs, 86'd from pizza parlors. It was his decibel level, his tactlessness. He was loud. There were always military families in earshot.

Finally, Luther called from outside of baggage claim. He had an extra suitcase with him. It was 6 p.m. He was wearing Lacoste.

"Was it worth missing Spring Fling?" Jihaad said. "Was it?"

"Later," Luther said. "Slow down, King, will you? This isn't NASCAR."

"We're late for something. It's a surprise."

Selma had conspired with The Lyceums to throw Lu-

ther a party, with girls. She ordered catering and a blue pi-
ñata in the shape of a lion, the Columbia mascot. She made
bean pies and promised that she and Delight would get lost
for a few hours.

"Tell me about the dance," Luther said.

"They wouldn't play any grinding music," King said.

Spring. Girl Scouts had *carte blanche,* thin mints. On
Hegenberger King weaved and fishtailed. The Lyceums
had different favorite Wayans Bros. They could read one
another's moods.

"It could have been worse. Some schools have their
proms at Richard Nixon's Library," Luther said. "They
dance on his grave."

"Who's that?" King said.

Back at the house Selma prepped for the party and
baited her breath. She hoped it wouldn't embarrass Luther.
She had taped up streamers with blow-ups of his baby photos. She invited Lyn.

Luther had been gone for ten days. The time differ-
ence threw Selma off. She couldn't get a hold of him when
she wanted. He had his "phone" off for much of it and pulling into the driveway – he was head-and-shoulders above
his friends, she didn't know where he got his brains or his
height – he looked different to Selma, wizened, as if he had
survived some tragedy. He had had a taste of it, Manhattan, an enormous bite. She had wanted a picture of him
at Ground Zero. She wanted a 'Proud Lion Parent' coffee
mug. The mood of the party was convivial but Luther was
not speaking very much to his guests, or audibly. There simply weren't any words for Lexington Avenue in the Eight-
ies on Sundays as the churches were dismissed, beers with

DiCaprio, hoops with Jeremy Lin, cockblocking Gosling at the Boom Boom Room. It actually happened, all of it. There was no equivalent and nobody would understand, with the exception of Delight who had been to New York but only for two days twenty years ago, holed up in the Hotel Diplomat, working. Selma's party was a labor, a slog. Luther dismissed congratulations and during the Apple-Bob (his favorite fruit) he hardly tried and quit after biting off a stem. A half-hour of this – the agenda of Lyn's long glances, King's MMA braggadocio – and Luther ducked out for air. The sun had not yet set. It was unsafe to walk unescorted, even for dudes, but he was tired of flying, sitting. He was a rogue flamingo, perfectly content with his own company, comfortable on one leg. Leaving JFK he had cried himself hoarse.

On their way to Luther's the Lyceums had evaded a DUI checkpoint set up near the Coliseum as the Athletics/Rays game was letting out. Four vehicles had been impounded and twelve drivers cited but ostensibly it was supposed to prevent these kinds of things from happening: one of Lyn's neighbors, who after sixteen pints was cut off in the 7th inning – Milo Ray Duer, 67, a Midwesterner by birth – jumped the curb at 56th and International as Luther waited for the *Walk* signal to cross. He was at that moment, had Duer seen him, an assured but not yet fulfilled young man, a future Rhodes Scholar, a future non-profit executive. His pants were low, half off, where they belonged. His underwear was visible. It wasn't a gang sign, it was layering. He had a paperback in his pocket, *The Long Valley*, an easy read by his standards, and a four-inch Leatherman which he used mostly to open boxes, and sometimes to cut the tags off of clothes.

Selma thought the cops at the door were trying to break up her party. "*It's not a rager, officer,*" she was about to say. "*We're spinning James Taylor.*" They opened with condolences. Luther had probably died instantaneously, they weren't certain except by the looks of it, which was no comfort to Delight, who heard these words through the fog of the motorcycle cop's visor, noting every scratch on it, not registering the gravity of it until Selma fainted on his arm.

She needed salts to revive her and injections to stabilize her. Had Luther survived he'd have refused painkillers. He was enterprising. He'd have sold them to his friends. He'd have let them autograph his casts.

::

After some vacillating and assurances from the mortician the Bartrams opened Luther's coffin up to mourners, who were queued up outside Saint John Coltrane behind velvet ropes. Luther was buried in his cap and gown. Selma tried not to lose it during the service. It was a memorial, not a funeral. She ran her fingernail along the mesh of his watch, like the chainmail of knights. She wanted to kiss his eyes. He was an organ donor.

Hearts went out, flowers by the dozens. In the middle of the eulogy the pastor broke down. Luther had kept every paper he wrote for school, he told the congregation, filed in order, A through F. He would have turned eighteen today, he said. At Skyline he should be enshrined.

A photo taken of Luther when he was fourteen circulated in the media. Selma was affronted. It didn't look any-

thing like the man he was growing into. Al Sharpton telephoned with his apologies. The Reverend Farrakhan sent a
letter with plans. They didn't know Luther but they referred
to him by first name and omitted the honorific.

"It's Mr. Bartram to you," Selma reminded the great men.

Her neighbors and people as far as Albany wanted to
cook for her, run her errands. Luther was an overnight hero,
a rallying cry, the Alamo, the Maine. There were candle-
light vigils, effigies. Vendors were selling RIP decals. It was
all too much. A script was in the works.

Delight and Selma were not public people. Their lives
had always been interior, without oomph. The community pillars were the retired bootleggers, the assemblymen,
the Rickey Hendersons. Selma did what she thought she
would have done when Luther would have left for college.
She started gambling online, smoking. They were doing it
all wrong, apparently. They were not vocal enough. They
did not turn Luther into a cause. They did not use him to
campaign against drunk driving, income inequities, gen-
trification. Where was Selma with Wolf Blitzer in a t-shirt
silkscreened with the 14-year-old Luther? Why had Delight
shut himself in, TV dinners with the television off, marathon games of Solitaire? It was an aberration. They were
accused of self-loathing, gossiped about. Luther must have
been gay, it was rumored. They must vote Republican.

Counsel from the NAACP met with Delight in a conference room in Oakland's City Center. They talked copyrights and merchandising. Might as well get some, they advised.

Selma's grief was astonishingly simple. She missed Luther. That was it. She missed him. When she wanted to talk

to him she couldn't. Her life was one less and her memory of him was a photo booth of still images, poses. His existence had entitled her to certain things she felt were not only inevitable but inalienable: grandchildren, long holiday weekends, being called over at the last minute to babysit.

Some nests empty voluntarily. Others … It was as dreadful as retirement. The Bartrams were not talking to one another less but in a different tense. Delight's changes were also small but abrupt. He stopped brushing his teeth twice a day. He masturbated into his socks.

"I feel responsible," Selma said.

"No."

"I invited that Vietnamese girl."

"Don't beat yourself up," Delight said. "That's religion's job."

He didn't need his name carried on. Bartram had no special meaning. The spelling was arbitrary. It wasn't supposed to move forward. They declined a United Negro College Fund-sponsored parade down Telegraph Avenue, which would start peaceably and devolve, Delight was certain, into an excuse to profane the police and loot downtown. They opened their own Luther Bartram Memorial Scholarship Fund instead. An editorial in the *Tribune* observed Luther's uncanny resemblance to the President, who was not the only ambitious Black man in America but the most visible.

That wasn't Luther. He had thought Obama was a poor example. He was anomalous that way.

::

Jihaad and King got matching tattoos of Luther's initials on their abs. They demonstrated on campus and were banned from graduation. It was not a suspension but a zero-tolerance policy. The administrators were firm, Caucasian. The Lyceums couldn't scam their way out of it. All they wanted was to walk, Jihaad said. They promised not to smuggle in any beach balls. They weren't in that mood, exactly.

For King it was the final straw. On Grad Nite, instead of camping out at Great America, he stayed up late in Jihaad's grandparents' basement with sizzurp watching swimsuit contests, Miss and Mrs. Americas, pornos stolen from Good Vibrations.

King was nocturnal. He had the better night vision.

"It's 3 a.m.," Jihaad said, his eyes blood-shot. "You're fucking with my circadians."

Hate was as strong as love and King caught himself daydreaming in it. Three had been a good round number, Musketeers, Stooges. Luther was the first one with a size 10 shoe, the first one to start shaving. His death was evidence of everything declining. The Bill of Rights was a joke. Inaugurations were sponsored by Pepsi.

"Sit tight for a minute," he told Jihaad. "Miss Guam intrigues me."

"What happens to the losers?"

"Don't you know? They put them up for auction."

King's eyesight was poor. He wanted to get even but he wasn't sure on who. It was pent up, it needed to be channeled and steered. It was like conceiving a child. The revenge had to be done spontaneously, in love.

"Look, you're not going to like this. I'm backing out of

tomorrow," Jihaad said.

King was channel surfing for phone sex. In the commercials the nipples were blacked out. There was something for everyone. He could even pay to sext.

"Tomorrow is today," King said.

"Luther wouldn't have wanted this. Remember, at the Coliseum, during Wu Tang? You get puffed up. Luther always talked us out of it."

"His parents aren't doing shit."

"We're not criminals," Jihaad said. "Criminals don't refer to themselves as criminals."

There were a string of upscale restaurants along Grand Avenue. The patrons were well-heeled. It was where the off-duty cops went to unwind. There were rarely ever gunshots. Jihaad was fast-forwarding though *Cheers* to the dirty commercials when King tossed a Beretta into his lap.

"I bought it off Craigslist," King said. "You owe me $60."

Jihaad had only fired on people in arcade games, on livestock hitting the ALT key in *Oregon Trail*. He was not like King. He didn't want to take it out on strangers. He would not scuttle his future like those old Volkswagens which doubled as artificial reefs.

"Why don't we just use our fingers under our shirts?" he said. "Better yet, let's steal a car. Or key the first Mercedes we find."

King was engrossed. He heard none of it.

"Ope! That girl is dope." King erupted. "Mariah. Mariah. Mariah. Quick, where's a pen?"

"Count me out."

"I need you."

"I want no part of it. There are better ways. Will you listen? She won't actually love you," Jihaad said.

King got down Mariah's digits on a spare Bible, in Corinthians. It was the only paper handy. Hopefully Mariah worked mornings.

::

Camino heralded its fifth year in business on Grand with a special, a $35 *prix fixe*. It was not as bourgeois as Commis or Meritage. Delight knew the proprietor from his days umpiring intramural softball. He and Selma were seated at a long communal table. The first course was squid with cucumber, paired with Gewürztraminer.

It was their 31st anniversary. Selma had put on her grandmother's pearls and a spritz of Chanel. Her jewelry amounted to baubles. Delight stole a bite from her plate.

"Husband tax," he said.

It was their first real dinner alone since Luther. It was a celebration and a formality. The tables were like those found in pubs, scratched upon, deep carvings. The management encouraged it.

"Luther was here," Delight said.

"How do you know?"

He lifted the carafe of water to show her.

"*Grouta Garbo*," he read. "*Potatoes au groutin*."

Selma dug her nails into his wrist. She cried immodestly.

"Please," Delight said. "People will think I beat you."

"It's my fault."

"No."

"I had to invite that Filipino girl."

"What's with all this 'woe is me?'" Delight said.

"I'm not being woe is me," she said. "You married *me*. Woe is you."

There were, like the lease on a new car, conditions that made old age possible and without which Selma would back out. She was listing them quietly to herself when the Emergency Exit behind Delight sprung open with a feeble, simpering alarm. A shot was fired into the ceiling. The chef was pistol-whipped.

The conditions were young people around her, progressively younger people she could compare to Luther.

King went table-to-table, demanding cash and valuables. He was urged to put his gat away. He spat on one woman.

"Too far," Delight said.

"'t up, nigger!" King said.

Selma waited patiently for her turn. Another condition was a kitchen large enough to bake in. Baking was her love language. Luther had been wrong. Her best was not bean pies, but chocolate chip.

FOURTH BORE

There was nothing angelic about it. If anything it was a demonic investment, a lark. Moira wired the Mitsubishi dealership six-figures for its most tricked-out food truck, with a promise to Xi that she wouldn't interfere, hands-off.

"I'm just the money," she told him. "It's your menu."

Xi was a Mandarin line-cook, a Morrissey lover who fervently abhorred America. At demonstrations he burned flags, spat on ROTC cadets in fatigues. It was a cultivated, practiced meanness. It was also his heritage. He adhered to a dialectic of gradualness, a zen pessimism.

"I belong in the kitchen," he told Moira. "Not all Chinese are math professors."

She had placed an advert in the *Chronicle*, not a request for proposals as much as a call for ideas on how to spend her money. Xi's response was a business plan handwritten on a cocktail napkin. Take-out was, he argued, the new formula for take-over. His earlier tenure at Millennium was designed for emerging vegan gastronomicas, all of whom had *emerged*, except for him.

"They not only don't pay you in restaurants," Xi said, "they want you to put your heart into it, ha!"

He had a confident belly, like Buddha, or Hitchcock.

"I won't grind you up," Moira promised.

On both sides of the Bay it was Michelin-quality mobile eats, the Wild West of cuisine. Of all the food trucks, Chairman Mao was the flagship. It sold hibiscus sorrels, monkfish braised in Coca-Cola.

"Wherever Mao goes, we go," Xi said. "Or else I go."

He hated Mao Zedong and channeled his hate into delectable nosh. Xi had a yen for revenge. Mao had shut down the film productions, Chinese cinema. He turned beloved directors into janitors.

"Mao has quite the audience," Moira said.

"Internet groupies," Xi said. "Chaing Kaisheck, now there was a great man."

"He was a fascist."

"That is not important. The food is everything. It taste fresh, yes?"

Xi had shipped Moira the recipes he proposed, the ingredients. She followed them step-by-step, using up every dish in her kitchen. Her family were guinea-pigs.

"Tastes like fascism," Moira said. "A Chaing truck might offend some people."

"Some people." Xi was incensed. "I want to offend everyone."

Moira could afford to. She hadn't earned her inheritance, not in the conventional sense. It came from her uncle Maurice, her mother's brother, after whom she had been named and who molested her for what Moira estimated was a just shy of a decade. They were not the best years but there was no getting them back. As an apology, Maurice wrote her into his will. Moira had done him a solid by keeping it to herself; she didn't want to embarrass him. Still, at his wake, when Maurice's extended family were invited to share their fondest memories of him, it was the silence that held. There were none.

"You have a family?" Xi asked.

"Most nights," Moira said.

"I'm gay."

"Who cares? This is San Francisco."

"It's more than that," Xi said.

He had contracted it, he explained, from a 'bear' ped-

dling Jello shots at the Lookout on Castro who, for more
than one reason, was a memorable lay. Xi's viral load was
under control but he still carried Band-Aids in his wallet.
His blood was a health-hazard. He preferred dull knives,
food that didn't need cutting.

"I don't care about your status," Moira said.

"So we're compatible?"

"I think you're my chef," Moira said.

It was the one word Xi had trouble with.

"Zeff?"

English, not as a way of thinking but as a language,
was easy for him to work in, but hard to figure out.

"Sh-eff," Moira said.

"*Ch*eff," he repeated.

She threw up her hands, a gesture that did not translate. In many dialects there was no equivalent.

::

It was a year of overdue infrastructure. The Willie
L. Brown Jr. Bridge from Oakland to Treasure Island had
opened on Labor Day. Caldecott's Fourth Bore also was
ahead of schedule.

Moira's Mitsubishi handled like an amusement park
ride that was thrilling twenty years ago. It had frightened
her at first, the bulk of it, the blind spots.

"Relax," her husband, Deion, said the morning Moira
pulled it out of the dealership. "Just pretend you're driving
the biggest black cock on the road."

Her pet name for the truck was Bertha. It was her
daughter's suggestion. Stark was seven years old. They had

adopted her from Cambodia during an inexplicable lull in its political turmoil, and at Siem Reap flying back to the States Deion chanted *Pol. Pot. Pol. Pot.* as he was pat down by security. The adoption process had been surprisingly smooth. It depended on the host country, apparently. Plus they weren't picky.

Moira did not divulge this to Xi. Her professional and personal lives did not overlap. Home life belonged at home, and there were joys to working that were singular to work, liberating even, like driving. It was her new outlet. She screamed at other drivers and used her horn indiscriminately. She flipped off Jettas. She started sleeping better.

Xi didn't have a car and he didn't believe in public transit. Moira picked him up on her way into the city. It was important to get into traffic early. On the 24 between Walnut Creek and Orinda there were flocks of wild turkeys, speed traps, deer.

"I was a good boy last night," Xi said. "At Moby Dick until 4, then Esta Noche." He wiped his eyes. "I can't keep coming in bloodshot."

He danced in cages, with poles. HIV was not a death sentence; he had almost forgotten what it stood for. In fact for some men, Xi was a fetish. Moira was intrigued by his fishnet blouses, his Fu Manchu. She had only seen them in cartoons. She grew up in a gated community, Rancho Santa Fe. She had no culture. Nothing offended her.

"Why Danville?" Xi asked.

"Pickpockets, cradle robbers," she said. "It's a dangerous world. Why Lafayette?"

It was curious to Moira why an unattached homosexual would not live in the city, but that was his business.

"I'm not sure what to expect today. There's a protest at Civic Center. The square can fit thousands. They'll be hungry," she said. "This could be the best September 11th ever."

"Second best," Xi said.

There was a hierarchy to his hate. Mao was 'hateful' or 'very hateful' or 'hateful indeed.' As was Nancy Pelosi, Oprah. He listed his hate in litanies.

"I've been reading up on Mao," Moira said.

Deion had recommended several books on what he called "Oriental" political developments, but she couldn't get a grip on it. The new China was too much like 1960's America to her, too reminiscent of Tiger Beat, Doris Day.

"I have too many books," she added.

"So do I. Like, twenty," Xi said.

Moira listened to the engine. She was OCD about the tire pressure. There was a bottleneck at the Caldecott.

"This gridlock," she exhaled. "Four lanes into two. A man designed this."

Moira didn't know who Caldecott was, didn't care. All she knew was that he was an asshole for only building three bores.

"You must love it," Xi said.

"Traffic?"

"You do it every day."

Like sparring partners they were getting to know another. Moira had studied investors and producers who, as the joke went, pissed in everyone's tomato juice. She swore she wouldn't, but when she got the opportunity to she couldn't resist. She bristled when Xi suggested more hybridity in the menu, more spice. He wanted to garnish his Hunan with grated radish and she didn't let him. He proposed that they park South of Market and she said no.

It was the only calendar she adhered to:

M 10:00-2:00 Fort Mason
T, Th 11:00-3:00 Octavia & Gough
W 2:00-5:00 Broadway & 12th (Oak)
F 10:00-4:00 UN Plaza
Sat 1:00-5:00 Embarcadero (Ferry Bldg.)

It was Mao's calendar, down to the minute. Chaing stalked Mao. The Siricha-crazed patrons were amused. Moira's was the Cadillac of foreign-made trucks. The roof was solar, the stovetop a revolutionary smokeless system of magnets.

There was success at first, then notoriety. She was told the cuisine was delicious but her palate, from years of smoking Virginia Slims, was shot. It was farm to table, hand over fist. In October Moira comped the critics and journalists; in November she bribed the health inspector. It didn't matter what color the curb was as long as the cops ate for free.

Xi was not a subordinate, but an equal. She could trust him with a stack of blank checks. She stood next to him all day but she only saw that one side of him, his profile, the left. He remained elusive to her. In previous kitchens he had failed personality tests – "a lack of narcissism," he explained.

They were intense months, yet calm. Xi was rationing himself. Work did not deserve all of him, especially not at night. Those were his best hours.

Watched pots, it turned out, did boil. Moira was getting rich in the modern way, not a windfall like the one

Maurice left her, but a dollar from everyone. She rarely ate her own fare. She didn't Twitter, either. Her food did the talking. It was meant to be photographed, not eaten.

::

Sunday mornings were sacred. Moira slept in. It was un-Momlike, unmaternal, lazy. She and Deion and Stark could go camping but did not. They window-shopped in downtown Danville and lunched in the family-friendly ale houses. Other families were in cafes, at the racetrack, in church.

It was early December. It wasn't just ale. There were grower champagnes for purchase at Finnegan's, aged ports. Moira and Deion started with Guinnesses. They did the crosswords, Sudokus. The pints stacked up. They didn't hide their drinking from Stark. It was important to start her out young.

"Spell 'esoteric.'" Deion said suddenly.

"D-o-n-t-i-n-s-u-l-t-m-e," Stark said.

She had shut her lips to sentences, sewn them. The Nor-Cal Bee qualifier was in two weeks. Stark had memorized Black's Law, back to front. Deion coached her but he didn't push her. The Bee was her dream, not his. It would be televised for the first time, on ESPN.

"It's no more a sport than golf is," Moira said.

"Wrong," Deion said. "Ironmans are easier."

He was always drinking, in sunglasses, perpetually hungover. Moira supposed it was better than meth or Ultimate Frisbee. He tried drying out in Oregon, in Palm Springs. The cures were expensive. They didn't take.

"Guinness is too light," Deion said. "Let's downshift into Moet."

It arrived on a cart, in an ice bucket. Moira didn't need it. She didn't like how she looked in bikinis. She was getting fat, sneaking up on diabetes. She was told she looked like a Moira when she wanted to look like a Rita, a Hedy, a Hepburn.

Deion poured three flutes. Stark liked listening to it fizzle. It sounded to her like the adult Rice Krispies.

"To the 1%," Deion toasted.

There was her money and his money. They had not merged accounts. Moira still had her maiden name. Most of Deion's work was not worthy of biography or becoming of the public servant he was. At the Water Board he had a Churchillian stamina for meetings and minutes. Moira had wanted him to be a lawyer – it was status, she could brag – but he couldn't seem to shrug off adversity. He saw adversity in his workplace, in preparing dinner, in washing his hands.

"It's Hanukkah. You know what that means," he said.

"C-h-r-i-s-t-m-a-s-t-i-m-e." Stark said. "T-i-m-e-t-o-b-u-y-m-o-m-a-L-e-x-u-s."

The 25th was also Moira's birthday. She asked for no parties, no tiara, just to lay low. She was turning thirty. Thirty terrified her. Most of her twenties had meant nothing. She had had the money, but she couldn't cash in.

"Spell 'egalitarian.'"

"P-l-e-a-s-e."

Stark was not a prodigy, but when they took her to the DeYoung or OMCA she focused on how smoke was painted, and glass. She gravitated to the Miros. She walked past the DeKoonings without pausing.

"Just think," Deion said, sipping from Stark's flute, "most people are drinking coffee right now."

She looked at him sternly.

"T-h-a-t-w-a-s-m-i-n-e."

"It's like a green light, kid." Deion mussed her hair, a bowl cut with bangs. "Just because you have it doesn't mean it's yours."

Sundays were liturgical, house to Finnegan's and then back again. It was a family ritual without detour. In the afternoon Deion mowed and weeded. Chores somehow turned into total disarray. Inside, the roses he had picked for Moira needed silica.

"The house is in squalor," Moira complained.

Sunday nights were the customary matrimonial pratfalls.

"W-h-a-t-i-s-f-o-r-d-i-n-n-e-r?"

"You're almost eight," Moira told Stark. "You're old enough to cook for yourself."

She was growing like a beanpole. Moira investigated ways to stunt her growth. She suggested espresso with her Flintstone vitamins. She did not want Stark playing basketball.

"C-a-n-w-e-h-a-v-e-f-a-s-t-f-o-o-d?"

"No, and I don't love what you've been eating after school."

It was an all-girls academy in Alamo. By fifth period Stark was starving. It was an open campus at lunch and she slathered her Happy Meals in condiments. She hoarded the packets. Mustards to her were shots of energy, quick fixes.

"Let her be a kid," Deion said. "She's metabolizing it. Think of all the shit we ate at her age. Velveeta, for instance."

"She's too smart to love McDonalds," Moira said.

Sunday nights were also for homework. Third grade was onerous. Stark was considering dropping out. She needed time to write her opus: NASCAR the Opera. Her instructors didn't pay much attention to her. They didn't think she needed it. Plus she never asked.

"Stark," Deion said, holding the remote. "Were you watching television earlier?"

"N-e-g-a-t-i-v-e."

"I thought I heard the Disney Channel."

"I-m-u-s-t-h-a-v-e-a-d-o-p-p-e-l-g-a-n-g-e-r."

She was a simple girl. She rode escalators for fun. She liked going down. There was also more to her than to most adults. Her bedtime reading was not the Boxcar Children, but Machiavelli. She could read tarot, ride unicycles. She knew jokes from Hustler.

::

In a way it was Moira's bore, her achievement. She had watched it from the start, read up on it, scrutinized the fact sheets. She had willed it into being. Its surface was smoother. It was brighter.

"Does it have a name?" Xi asked.

"Number 4," she said.

"At what cost?"

"Couple hundred mil. It's just bond money."

"And it'll save you, what, 12 minutes a month?"

It was still a savings. It wasn't always thrilling, this life. Moira had wanted it all to be seismic, but even earthquakes sometimes underwhelmed her. Life was premium grades of gasoline, how to squeeze a cantaloupe. It was also vehicular. Bertha was not a smooth ride but she turned heads. She and Xi got closer, commuting together. It was almost bonding. When the weather changed and she got the sniffles he suggested homeopathic remedies like dry socks over wet socks, vapor rubs on her feet, which were wives' tales he admitted but *working* wives' tales. He asked her questions about America in a way that led her to believe he was relaxing his animosities. He was especially fascinated by the riff between the sexes.

"Rift," she corrected. "T-*uh*."

"Too many divorce-*tuh* Americans."

Xi looked sicker to her of late, more anemic. He was taking a holiday from his drug cocktail. Lost weight was a side-effect.

"You're against marriage?"

"Everyone's doing it," he said. "It's not special anymore. I can't even find anyone to sleep with me. I don't mean sex, but actual sleep."

"Ah, sleep. In our marriage …"

Xi interrupted.

"From the way you talk, I can't tell who's the husband."

Work wasn't her blood and it wasn't her sweat and tears. Moira began to wear aprons while Xi switched to Crocs, like Batali. Chaing wasn't a franchise truck like Mao. Moira would not soft-launch trucks in New York or Austin. There was no cookbook in the works. All of the recipes were in Xi's head.

He had taught her a little Chinese. Moira got a grip on its cultural tethers, the faith in ghosts, the primacy of family. Meanwhile, the pace was breakneck. They expanded to

Noe Valley, a pocket of artifice between the infill skyscrapers and Victorians. On weekends she catered weddings, bar mitzvahs. They parked Chaing outside wineries and construction sites. It was sensory and it was calories, stripped-down fare. She wasn't hallucinating. It was that good.

"I don't get it," Xi announced during a smoke break. His foot was resting on Bertha's bumper. "I don't get how you can have Giants *and* Athletics stickers. You can't cheer for both. It's not like you want Chaing and Mao to *both* win. This kind of shit just seems impossible."

"I can't afford to take sides," she said.

She was a small business owner in every sense of the word: cutting corners, writing off perms and pedicures as business expenses. She could find the silver lining in human excrement. Her profanity was chaste, *Holy Mole, Holy Toad*. Her prayers were appeals to the wrong patron saints.

On an uninspired Wednesday, as the trucks were packing up and racing back to Alameda, Xi poured granulated sugar down Mao's fuel tank, followed with a jar of hoisin sauce.

"The sweet with the savory," he explained.

People were swine to him. They fit into two categories: homebodies and antibodies. He had to be able to joke about it. It was more than a tear in a condom or deviantism. He had found closure by not shutting himself down. There were others with HIV who were thriving in spite of it, but to do so took money. Not everyone was Magic Johnson. There were the Tommy Morrisons, the Rock Hudsons, the deniers.

"Oh, fuck," Xi uttered one afternoon.

He had flensed his palm scoring jalapenos. He sucked on the wound. There were droplets of blood on the cutting board -- five, Moira counted, as if from an eyedropper.

It was Chaing's rush-hour. She apologized to every-one queued up. They had to close for the day. It was not an emergency, she said, but ... they had run out of secret ingredients, and paprika.

"Let me," Xi said, as Moira sanitized the board.

"I got it."

There was no mess of his she wouldn't happily clean up. She tossed out the dish-rag and then, as if on second thought, the cutting board and the paring knife and her apron.

"It's not airborne," Xi said.

"I know."

"I'm sorry."

"Don't be."

"It's a gay cancer."

"You can't say that," she said. "Do not say that."

There were disclosure rules Moira had not adhered to. The new revolution was more government, all government, but she refrained. No-one needed to know.

::

The family tree went up, a twelve-foot Douglas Fir. All year they had stockpiled ornaments. To Moira, it was the season of giving and of giving people headaches.

Deion's loving gestures increased. It was the 12th and they were behind on their Advent Calendar. She found him waiting on the porch for her to come home, clutching an arrangement, a bouquet she did not recognize.

"What is this?"

"Poinsettias," he said.

"You only get me flowers anymore," she said.

The Bee was in seventeen hours. Stark lugged her around dictionary around the house. Her focus had not flagged even though she had asked for fencing gear for her next hobby, a foil, an opponent. Deion was against all of it. It wasn't like the spelling circuit. There was no competition to demolish.

"Time to limber up your alphabet," Deion announced.

She would have a hard time with boys. The Bee wouldn't get her anywhere, Moira knew, into Harvey Mudd maybe, but not into the Homecoming court. It was better just to undo all she had learned.

That evening they carb loaded on pasta as if she was about to run a marathon. Before bedtime Stark told a recess fib Moira saw straight through. It cost her her nighttime reading, a biography of Robert E. Lee. She cried into her pillow.

"It was a small lie," Deion said.

"When her lies start carrying more weight, she'll get better at telling them," Moira said.

They were sitting upright in bed, with cocktails, watching silent films on mute. It was a junior-master bedroom with vaulted ceilings, a California King. Stark had the master-master.

"Want another one?" Deion asked.

"A Negroni? No, too bitter," Moira said.

"Not that," he said. "Another Stark."

It was the advantage of adoption. There was nothing to pass down. Stark had been spared whatever it was in Moira's blood that yielded to her uncle. 'Molestation' was a big enough word and Moira used it so she didn't have to be specific and shudder again recalling fellating Maurice in the Applebee's parking lot, or the upholstery rashes, or the rug-burns. She had been, otherwise, a quite normal girl, nuclear even. The *Wonder Years* were on primetime and when Joey from New Kids From The Block kissed her hand she didn't wash it for a week. Maurice fit no profile she was aware of. He hadn't been creepy about it. He had charmed her and then forced himself.

"You never told me any of this," Deion said.

"It's all this talk of children."

"I can't imagine how you feel."

"Somehow it was more wondrous then," she said.

"When did it stop?"

"I grew a pair one night," Moira said. "I made him undress first and then I kicked him in the nuts. And then I got his testicles in a vice-grip."

"And what did he do?"

"He submitted. 'The one day you don't wear a jock-strap,' he joked. He never lost his sense of humor."

Moira still had Maurice's number in her phone. Now that he was dead he no longer owed her, he was no longer beholden.

"I'm making you another drink. I'm speechless for once," Deion said. "Can I give you a massage?"

"It's funny," Moira said. "They die and then you have to pay the newspaper for an obituary. 'A predator is dead,' I told the editor. 'This is news. You pay me.'"

She had been in Maurice's hospice room near the end. His last breath was more of a heave. It wasn't easy – she had to squat – but eventually she urinated on his grave, in broad daylight, in spanx. She had sworn to.

::

"Twirl for your mother," Deion directed Stark.

The girl obliged, frowning. They were in the foyer, where the coats were kept.

"Don't you like your new dress?"

It was from TopShop, bought by Moira especially for the Bee, with sequins. It was pink.

"T-h-i-s-c-o-l-o-r-d-o-e-s-n-o-t-f-l-a-t-t-e-r-m-e."

"Perk up kid," Deion said. "You look sullen."

"I-t-i-s-j-u-s-t-n-e-r-v-e-s."

She was seeded second. Deion tried to bet on the outcome, to find odds, but had failed. No book was taking action, not even Cache Creek, which placed odds on everything, from the name of Prince William's son (George went off at 4-1) to Pope Francis (75-1).

The venue was the Oracle Arena, in Oakland. They took the family sedan.

"I-c-o-u-l-d-n-t-s-l-e-e-p-l-a-s-t-n-i-g-h-t."

"Look, your father was in a bar fight," Deion said. "His septum is deviated. He snores."

"Y-o-u-a-l-s-o-g-r-i-n-d-y-o-u-r-t-e-e-t-h."

It was Stark's first time through the new bore. By age five she had shook hands with the Clintons, walked across the Brooklyn Bridge. The bore was bright but it didn't merit comment. It took a lot to impress her.

Oracle was intimate enough for basketball and for Yanni concerts. As a sporting event the Bee was climbing the charts. There were tailgaters in the parking lot, scalpers.

In the Creekside Lot their car alarm went off.

"Beep beep beep," Deion joked.

"I-n-s-t-e-a-d-o-f-m-i-m-i-n-g-i-t-w-h-y-d-o-n-t-y-o-u-f-i-x-i-t?"

Oracle was in the shadow of the Coliseum, an afterthought of the national pastime. Inside there were clowns and face-paint and jugs of horchata for the children. Stark found some friends of hers in the audience and busied herself by curating a series of selfies. The platinum sponsors were Harborside and Oaksterdam, the marijuana dispensaries. Wineries from Napa and Livermore had set up booths.

"My love," Moira said, rubbing Deion's shoulders, "thank you for being the envoy of the marriage and putting your liver in the line of fire."

Like most alcoholics Deion had an intolerance to all drugs, even pot. He preferred to talk about wine, to know and speak of the great houses intimately.

"This isn't a wine," he said, sampling one. He was sensitive to weak pours. "It's a label."

"Robert Parker called it 'Sophia Loren in a glass,'" the winemaker countered.

"More like Twiggy, without the legs. Try it," he said to Moira.

"I'll pass."

"Why are you so averse to zinfandel?"

"I'm like that with all reds," she said.

The incompatible ESPN announcers were seated behind the judges' table. At the appointed time Stark and the fifteen other contestants ran onto the hard-court to *Welcome to the Jungle*, high-fiving Stomper, the elephantine A's mascot, because the Warriors had fired theirs. In the cheap seats ecstatic parents cheered with noisemakers, foam fingers. The emcee, a Berkeley physicist, cracked Oppenheimer jokes.

In round-robin format, the Bee began. Stark's contestant ID was on upside down. Her peers quickly thinned. The sixth seed from Country Day went out on 'absquatulate.' The first seed, the 2012 champion, forgot the first 'e' in 'resupinate.'

Stark was still standing. She worked her way deftly through 'genethliac' and nearly omitted the 'h' in 'witzelsucht.' After an hour it was just her and the 16th seed, a Pakistani girl from Julia Morgan's School, standing at half-court in an actual spotlight. It was sudden death. Like Frasier-Ali, they traded blows. Stark clasped her hands behind her back. Neither girl flinched.

"Your word is ketchup," the proctor told Stark. "Ketchup. Would you like the definition?"

Stark smiled. It was her favorite. It was slam-dunk. She nodded.

"A tasty red sauce, or a thick sauce, made with tomatoes, that is served cold as a condiment. Origin, Chinese. Noun."

Stark shut her eyes. There were dozens of packets in her desk at school. She was visualizing it.

"Catsup," she said. "C-a-t-s-u-p. Catsup.

The judges conferred.

"I'm sorry," the emcee announced.

Where the other contestants, after having faltered, nodded and passively walked off court, Stark held her ground.

"You tried," the emcee consoled her. "Effort." He put a hand on her shoulder. "It counts."

An anemic round of applause started up. Stark reached for the microphone. She was on her tip-toes.

"Cunts," she said.

Oracle was unsure of what it had heard. Except for Deion's laughter there was silence.

"C-u-n-t-s. Cunts."

It was the correct spelling. Stark stormed off court. They didn't stick around for the runner-up trophy. She had plenty at home.

::

Moira's alarm clock was a soft, simpering chime. The bathroom window faced the street and the garbage men tried to get glimpses of her showering. She got ready stealthily, so as not to wake everyone. She checked in on Stark to kiss her goodbye.

"Mom," Stark said.

"What is it? A nightmare?"

"Not really."

She was a normal child again. She was using words..

"Talk to me," Moira said. "Don't stop talking."

"It was a dream. In this dream we were at the bank and the teller was on hold trying to help Dad, but then I woke up."

"Ok."

"So what happens to him?" Stark asked.

"Who?"

"The teller. He was so helpful. I woke up. Now he's just frozen there."

Moira envied her daughter. She had something to dream about. Her dreams weren't Maurice.

::

That morning Moira picked up Xi, as usual. He wasn't talkative. She turned the radio to the AM. It was talk radio, televangelists.

"Did Stark win?"

She would allow Stark to be brokenhearted. She would let her fence. It was one of the lessons she had learned waiting for Maurice to tire of her, or kick the bucket: there was always a day *after* the day she never thought would arrive.

"She won," Moira said. "Where were you last night?"

"I'm in no shape to party," Xi said. "I'm sick."

"You sound fine."

"I've lost eighty pounds. You can't tell?"

She could, and did. There was a convexity to Xi. She wasn't sure whether to express concern, or, depending on his fitness goals, congratulate him.

"It's just that I see you every day," she said.

"It's worse," he said. "It's full-blown."

Xi was in Arthur Ashe territory now. It was how he lived, as a bottom, a passenger. He was along for the ride.

"My eyes are crossing," Moira said. "Want to drive?"

She had reflexively taken the third bore, instead of the fourth. Caldecott was more than a conduit, just as Bertha was more than a conveyance. It was a divide. Her side of the tunnel was the money side where the affluent people lived longer: that was the price.

"For real?" Xi asked.

She pulled over at the Broadway exit.

"I've been in charge long enough," she said.

To her surprise he was a good driver. He sat tall in the driver's seat. She had never seen this side of him. He used his mirrors.

As they approached Civic Center the other food trucks had already formed a half-moon facing City Hall. Moira rarely tired of it. It was, framed by the barren mulberry trees strung with icicle bulbs, a California Christmas, the quintessential Tenderloin.

"I'll let you out here," Xi said, pulling up to a bodega.

"It's right there," Moira protested.

"I just ... I need pack of smokes, please."

Moira hopped out of Bertha holding a crumpled five as Xi gassed it. His personality had failed again. Mao had done his family an unspeakable wrong. Bertha was the perfect vehicle to get even.

Like Xi, like Stark. Time bombs went off on their own time. Xi increased his speed, jumping curbs. His aim hadn't wavered. The Mao employees scurried. He couldn't miss.

Moira wished she had such courage. Her emotional marrow was not that vast. It needed mining and naming but she wasn't sure what to call it. In high school she had had a Karmann-Ghia named Jane, trading it in after college for Chevrolet Bel-Air she named Susan B. in celebration of all women – w-o-m-y-n.

Aldo came home tired but talkative. It's what made the house bearable.

"The Dow closed at the top of the charts, 3,061, which is about how many days since it rained. I short-sold Clorox when it dropped six cents and we netted $12,000. How was your day? Congratulate me," he said.

Marti shrugged. She couldn't confidently say.

Aldo unlocked his briefcase. The inside lining was torn. She had packed him leftovers, untouched. He checked the hygrometer.

"It's humid downstairs."

"I know. It beeped," she said.

"It'll mold. You don't want that."

She didn't want any of it. Sometimes she thought it was why he married her, for her inheritance of framed jerseys, pennants, signed baseballs she wasn't allowed to touch.

"It can't mold," Marti said. "It's behind glass."

"Did you check for vapor?"

"I had a million things to do," she said, trying to remember exactly what. Most days she had to make a list to convince herself she had been productive. *Cleaned disposal*, she wrote. *Changed bulb*.

She was changing her allegiance from Gov. Clinton to Jerry Brown when Aldo started to talk retirement. At first it was something he ventured over dinner with his fork in the air, a distant thing, a marathon in Antarctica. It scared her when he brought it up. She wasn't sure what he was like during the day.

Her forties had been tidy so far, tamely exciting. Trips to Cabo, to Palm Springs, the poor man's Cancun. She wasn't like her friends who lived off campus near Cal, dissipated, obsessed with PBS, Birkenstocks. She found it unbearable going to their houses, cluttered, vibrant with children. She envied their problems, their concurrences of disaster, divorces and affairs, bouts of chicken pox.

It was Wednesday. Marti poured Aldo a drink, his first of four. He puckered.

"You've been overbittering my Gibsons," he said.

"It's arsenic," she said.

She was as thin as she was at 27, her hair a shade grayer than Emmylou Harris.' Aldo had no body image issues. He was soft and his hair had thinned finely and she found a mole on his neck inspecting him for melanoma in the shower.

Tuesdays were taco nights. On Wild Card Wednesdays they hardly ate. Marti turned on the TV as Aldo trained his telescope on the neighbors. It was a Desi and Lucy re-run. She wondered in which of the twin beds they had made Ricky. She waited.

It was everything she wanted, on paper: a big house on stilts in the Hiller Highlands with a pioneer's view and a yard populated with Rain Bird sprinklers which, like the eucalyptus, were not indigenous to the area. Aldo had worked so hard for it, adding on in '88 with his bonus. (*'That's the great thing about money,"* he loved to say. *"A lot of it goes a long way."*) They weren't as high up as the senior partners, but they could see the Transamerica and San Quentin through the telescope, and the two ballparks, the Coliseum and the 'Stick, on the few nights out of every month when it was unobstructed bliss. Six out of seven it was fog encroaching and darkness, folding on itself.

Like the view, Aldo isolated his libido to one day a

week. It was a big bed, a California King, wide enough for
them to never touch.

He squinted and swiveled the scope toward downtown
Oakland. Marti missed her life down there, Seventh-Day
solicitors and ice cream truck songs and the faint prospect
of burglary, her clotheslines and scrappy gardens and anemic romanesco and the neighbors who would wait until sun-
down to steal their plums. And walking: when they moved
into the Oakland Hills her legs had turned to cheese. From
sitting. From nothing.

"Come here," Aldo motioned, doubled over the tripod.

"I don't want to watch anyone fucking," Marti said.

"Trust me."

He was spying on the Stearns, who lived a few thousand yards down on the Berkeley side. The husband was
ironing; something was smoking. Marti thought she should
go over one afternoon, introduce herself.

"What am I looking at?" Marti asked.

"She's breastfeeding," Aldo said. "You can't see it?"

In their late twenties he might have had a child with
her, had she said only said the word. They had words for
things in those days, and friends, and a code for exiting droll
parties. Then his language for children changed. '*It's crying*,"
he'd say, holding a colleague's newborn. "*Take it away.*"

"What don't you see?" Aldo asked.

Marti refocused the lens. She wondered what they said
to one another. What they could possibly say.

"Infertility?" she said.

"A liquor cabinet," Aldo said. "It's a dry household."

The world wasn't flat, but he talked like it. People
who didn't drink couldn't have the same problems, or any

problems worth talking about. His life was a big band and the cocktail shaker was the rhythm section. Marti's eye was glued. The Stearns had an open floor plan, very modern. She read a tabloid as she pumped. They looked to Marti like churchgoers, godfearers. As the child motored around he sidled up to her and fed on her other breast, snarling as he bit. It was a high-end scope. Marti could see, vividly, her stretchmarks, milk in his beard.

People fascinated Marti. As organisms. Not as people.

::

October was a caramel epoch. The drought had dried out the eucalyptus and there was a hard wind, a foehn wind that blew lupin and oleander all over her porch. Marti waited all year for this time of year. She looked forward to baking pumpkin bread, reserving a bird at the butcher's. She was not looking forward to Christmas, when she wanted to hear Bing and Aldo played Elvis. Halloween was her favorite holiday. She didn't have to be her, for once.

Marti, short for Marcia. Short for martial law. She was not self-centered. She just had nothing else to discuss. When she tried new things Aldo reversed them. She tried volunteering. She grew out her bangs. For a week she was a crossing guard. He made fun of her spiritual quests and chakras. He laughed at her finding herself.

In '86 she got a male Labrador, a rescue she renamed Avery. Aldo decided he would make a good guide dog. There were a series of tests Avery had to pass. Marti issued him commands and protocols until she was no longer conversant with humans. At his graduation he was given to a blind kid from Phoenix who tripped over the leash.

It was an age of euphemism, 1991, of naming things what they were not. Wife was partner. Turbulence was unstable air. Aldo still went out Thursday nights, in paisley and smelling of Old Spice, chest hair showing, looking rich. When he was out drinking he felt 25. The next morning he was 45 again. Oats needed sowing.

"Wish me luck," he said. "This could be the night."

"It won't work. They won't talk to you," Marti said. "You're married."

He looked at his band, a soft gold, dull and old.

"That's only legal in Georgia."

Then again, there were worse things than cheating. She knew she wouldn't divorce him; it was too much paperwork. As he let out the e-brake and backed down the driveway Marti didn't give a start or feel inexplicable pains or a cosmic vacancy. She felt annulled. For revenge, she pictured him alone at the bar shooing away imaginary flies. It was on one of these weeknights decades ago that she met Aldo. She was twenty, dolled-up, war paint. Around her neck was a locket without anyone in it, just a picture of a house, her dream house, gables, closer to her clavicle than her heart. She had been so confident then, politically riveted, socially liberated. Palpably terrified.

::

The penalty for elopement is no photos and an illicit feeling, like the wedding never happened. Those first months together in Fernandina she loved sex on bean-bag chairs, on waterbeds and the taut mesh between the hulls of his catamaran. She was a sophomore at Jacksonville State, crushing on her professors, a weakness for tweed. In the library she had to stamp her legs awake, her eyes tired, left to right for hours. Cognitively dissonant. She was the groupie cajoling security to let her backstage, donuts in parking lots, learning to drive stick. Her tan was tantalizing, her chic venomous. The ends of her sentences trailed. She never needed to finish anything.

She fell in love with Aldo because women were his natural companions and he had danced with the ugly girls at Prom. She didn't know what she was getting into. His phone calls were complex things with many parts, hard to put together. He was nervous for a Floridian, especially for one who surfed. Marti suggested pot. When he smelled it on her, inevitably on her clothes or in a pocket of air in the backyard, she blamed a skunk.

Her father and Aldo had more in common. They talked sports, salaries, draft picks. They debated fluctuations in attendance and announcers and the Kansas City franchise moving west. The old man used to wake her up at night, turning loud double plays in his sleep. He went to trade shows, expos, queued up at folding tables with greying shortstops signing foam fingers. It was a curious adolescence and there was something aristocratic about their impoverishment. She suffered hand-me-downs, second-hands – the indignity of a Datsun for her first-car – as with what would be her allowance he bought his foul-pole segments, his bleacher seats and chalk-encrusted ephemera and commemorative plates.

When he got cancer the first time he told her to treat the history like her pension, her siblings. He kept it in the attic, a humidified sanctum that smelled like her friends' parochial school, the nuns. There was Honus Wagner's (she pronounced it *V*agner) mitt and Christy Mathewson's resin bag, the home base Jackie Robinson stole and a replica of the actual house Ruth had built.

She thought it all should be in a museum. She didn't know who these people were. Most of them were dead, had to be.

Aldo came by the house more often once the chemo started, Sunday breakfasts to keep her father's spirits up. He was infirm. His blood was virtually dust. If Marti had known it was in his prostate, she'd have had him walk her down the aisle. She'd have let him pay for the whole wedding, instead of sneaking off to Georgia, signing the papers in Alpharetta, drafting the city clerk as a witness.

"Catch the one-hitter last night?" her father asked Aldo.

"I was in the car. Listened to it, though. Rollie threw a gem."

"Who?" Marti said. "Is he with the Mets?" She was tired of conversation just happening around her.

"Rollie Fingers. You know," Al said. "With the moustache."

She was quiet.

"You know who that is," her father said. "Don't play dumb."

He held the sports page over her breakfast. He could name most of Mantle's mistresses, all of Artie Shaw's wives. Marti twirled the house around her neck as she snuck glimpses of the box-scores, the player photos.

"Mr. Fingers needs a facial hair stylist," she said.

The men chuckled. It won her points.

::

She drew lines through the cities Al proposed, thick red lines through Omaha and Salt Lake City, even the places she didn't necessarily object to. Oakland was the last town standing. All Marti knew about California was Hollywood, fires, earthquakes. She wanted to be in pictures. She worried they would fall into the sea.

Al found work in a financial services firm in San Francisco, off Sansome. There was no playbook on how to move across the country. They loaded up a Bekins and bought a tract home across the bay in Montclair, then a rental property on Piedmont Ave., with the two good schools (Egbert Beach and Oakland Tech) and a Tiki bar nearby. It scared her that they were turning into *that* couple, living carefully, heavily insured, with an island in the kitchen and skylights and clear retirement goals. Al had become what she expected him to, a middle manager, terminally mature, 30 at age 26 and 50 by his 41st birthday. Instead of mountain biking – the terrain was great for it – he patronized the symphony. Instead of hiking he did the crossword.

As he got wealthier he lost the casual thoughtfulness Marti had come to expect: the impromptu flights to Vegas, the one rose on Valentine's for every year of marriage. When her father died in '77, more of Al's life moved around baseball. He had the memorabilia flown into SFO and met it at the airport. Christie's appraised it at $1.1 million. In '79 he moved her into one of the houses she dogeared in *Architectural Digest*.

She liked that it had a tree-house, twenty feet up the spruce with a ladder bolted to the tree. In the happy pictures of them she hammered into the walls there seemed room for a third person or a fourth, as if someone, small people, had been cut out. Al built a swimming pool that he never filled, and put up a shake roof because it was vogue. He threw out the hydrangeas before they went bad. A commentator said take more baths, longer ones: Marti did: Al bitched about the utility bill. He was suddenly afraid of flamboyant ties, paisley, Volkswagens, anything *fun*, which was so unlike his comportment around their old friends, the social workers and dee-jays in East Oakland who loved him and how defensive he was about his accent and his fascination at their refined marijuana palate. They could name the region the bud was grown in, the vintage. They laughed when Al stopped toking and talked over their heads and voted Reagan. He started using their code one or two drinks in, just as Marti was starting to have fun. He was acting 60, 62. He wasn't coming back.

::

MTV was kind to her when *Dallas* ended and she needed a new guilty pleasure. That solved her primetime problem. Weekdays were storms she waited out playing bridge over the phone and radios on in every room on different stations, bebop in the kitchen, R&B in the loo. She needed noise. Only the clocks were synchronized.

The A's were Al's outlet. He had been in favor of their move from Kansas City, and when the Royals released Bo Jackson Al went around the house breaking No. 2 pencils over his head and knees. Soon he had season tickets and was driving to Spring Training in Arizona to meet the prospects. Marti rarely joined him: road trips made her carsick: she didn't understand the desert or places like it. She was a sea-level creature. Why anyone would just golf their life away.

She would have been happy had the sports stayed out of her house, in a storage unit or on display at the Ferry Building. Her name would have meant something – *Donated Through the Beneficence of Marti Breems.* She had no say. In '82 with his promotion Al moved her things out of the basement and started renovating: glass enclosures and ventilation for the collection. He installed two deadbolts and, in the hallway three steps from her father's urn, a gauge with a magnetic remote, the hygrometer, so he could follow the temperature. He checked it as often as he did the knobs on the stove, just in case Marti had left them on.

It was Friday and the Stearns' windows were dark. After his third Gibson she found Al downstairs, talking to himself, dusting.

"We need to talk," he told her. "Upstairs."

He came up holding a rag with a blue smudge, and a Polaroid of a wall joint with vague dots.

"I told you," Al said, cupping the fabric. "Mold."

She almost giggled. His face was so severe for this – this small revelation.

"Where?"

"On the Mathewson."

"You had me scared for a minute," she said.

"It means there's too much moisture."

"As long as it's not in the walls."

Their voices were calm. Everything around them was orderly, clean.

"You suck at this," he said evenly. "Go see for yourself."

The stairs down were steeper than those up to the second and third floors. It was his domain. She hadn't seen it in years. The lights were soft. It was cool inside, like sunrise.

Looking around infuriated her. These things, the batting gloves and the felt pen autographs, they should be like people: allowed to deteriorate, lose value.

She had married her father.

So there was mold. She was no less important. She was just as well kept up. No plastic surgery yet. Mint condition.

Marti stormed up. In one hand she held a cap with an embroidered *R* and sweat stains. She didn't know whose it was. In the other she held garden shears. Al laughed, segregating her humor. Marti was all hyperbole. Always kidding around.

She put the bill between the steel. It was old cardboard. Flimsy. It was old hat.

Al's face changed. "That's priceless," he said.

"I swear I will."

He never said he didn't want children with her. But he didn't poke holes in the condoms. He never sabotaged her birth control. He didn't try.

"God, that's worth so much money."

He couldn't not invoke God. She would show him. She could escalate.

"That's a vacation to Europe," Al said.

She didn't know how or why it all survived. It wasn't even art.

"Say something nice," she said.

He would have to mean it. She could tell. There was no talking her down.

"I regret not having married you sooner," he said.

Al took a step at her. Two steps. She backed up. It was patently, cherry tree false.

::

Al tried not speaking to her the next morning. Marti could see him pretending to be upset. He was a bad husband and a worse actor.

At noon she got out of her pajamas and into sparkling wine. Migraines had sidelined her for most of his work parties. This one was different. He insisted that she go, for appearances' sake. It was a costume party, a dress rehearsal for Halloween. She couldn't decide between gray and blue, the frock or the boobs.

On 24 he tuned into the ballgame. It was the Series; the Twins were up. They merged onto 80. Marti still felt nervous on the Bay Bridge, all bridges. She sat stiffly. She never thought she would ever wear leather pants, a shirt off the shoulder. Her bra showing.

"Where's this party?" Marti asked.

"Aqua," he said.

She had read about it in *Food and Wine*. The wine list Al could never slay, not in two lifetimes.

"I'm allergic to shellfish," Marti said.

"Tonight you're not," Al said.

He was lively as he checked his bomber's jacket with the hostess. "It's the hollandaise season," he sang, snapping his fingers in the foyer, jonquil as a bee.

He was supposed to be James Dean. They were not early but the party seemed to her to be awfully thin. Al dove into conversations, drinking, clapping colleagues so firmly on the back that Marti worried about their toupees. He was on his second drink and shot back his third with a lime chaser.

She fished the keys out of his pocket. He was no good at driving drunk. He was no good.

Marti went to the bar, did a lap, flirted a little. People were a welcome sight, anyone.

"What is that you're drinking?" Al asked her. He sniffed above her glass. "Tequila?"

Marti didn't usually drink tequila. Tequila was a pants-opener.

"Come meet Lindsay and Phil," Al said. "Don't worry, you'll like her."

It didn't matter if she didn't. Phil was tall, regal. Lindsay was a guitar riff, shapes in her stockings, big earrings, neon.

"She's bad Sandy," Phil said. "From *Grease*."

"That's who Marti's trying to be," Al said.

There had been declines on Phil's desk, losses. It was like sticking with a losing coach. The interns took bets on how large the number was. In the scuttlebutt it became a mythical, legendary sum.

"Old Al knows as this is my last company party that I get to make a speech." Phil tapped the rim of his flute. "Fifty million dollars ago …"

"Let's not talk money," Lindsay said.

"Could happen to anyone," Al said.

"We're sunk. The traders need ethics training and the lawyers need drama classes. The Chinese are better off, the Russians." Phil motioned for a refill. "Who needs censorship when you've got capitalism?"

Lindsay turned to Marti. Had they met in college they would have been friends, slutting it up Friday nights, succumbing to peer pressures, karaoke.

"How's your son?"

Marti felt vacant, confused.

"I swear you had a son somewhere. Al, didn't you say you had a son? College age?"

Marti grabbed his forearm, dug her nails in.

"Would you believe it?" Al said, lilting. "He got into Stanford with a 92 on his verbal and a 31 on his math."

::

She didn't know how long she had been in the elevator. She felt herself going interminably up. On the roof she looked up and sighed. The moon was out, an Ichabod Crane moon. Al had tipped the maitre'd fifty bucks for the access key.

"I hate this," Marti said. "I hate this 'whose costume has the bigger dick.'"

She had felt nervous downstairs, nauseous. At any moment everyone would swap spouses, like musical chairs.

"Cosmonaut," she said.

"I always hated that word," Al said.

"Cosmonaut."

"It doesn't work anymore," he said.

"I said it. I get to leave." Marti spat. "How *is* our son?"

"You're fucking up. Who are you tonight? Fucking crazy."

"I'm drunk." She sighed, helplessly. "Lost control for once. And if the stray *hors d'oeuvre* made it into my gullet, so what?" She felt her hips. "No harm done."

"Breathe," Al said.

"Does he live on or off campus?"

"Look, slow down. We can't both be drunk."

"We'll take a cab home," Marti said. "What's his name?"

"I forgive you. Ok? I'll forgive you in the morning."

"You said we had a son? You fuck."

Al was disappointed in the venue. There were small things the piano player could do. Like play Sinatra. Wear a tux.

"I didn't say we didn't," he said. "Everyone else has one."

She was furious. Things had come in threes before. But never in the same weekend.

::

They had to walk to Mission and Fifth to find a cab. Marti lost her bearings. San Francisco was not a playground as Jacksonville had been; she hadn't learned any more about it than she had first time watching *Vertigo*.

The same was true of Oakland. It was a snake charmer. She didn't know it at all. She could have learned it, with a stroller. First steps. Look both ways. At intersections: Stop. Hammertime.

The driver looked at his *Thomas Guide*. He lived on Treasure Island. He didn't know the East Bay. His medallion was new.

"How old is Lindsay?" Marti asked.

"I don't know. However old she is, she looks it. They're swingers," he said.

"Yeah?"

"Just saying," Al said.

"That's gross."

"Why? Happily married people have affairs."

"Not you," she said.

She knew he couldn't. Not Al. Al knew what side his

butter was breaded on.

"I had plenty of chances," he said. "Did you know the Claremont Hotel has hourly rates?"

"For you, half-hourly."

The fare was at $14 and climbing. It was a fleet car; the rips in the seats were duct-taped. Al asked the driver to turn down the radio. Between the Broadway and College exits he was quiet. It made her uncomfortable, his thinking.

"If I was in jail," he said, "and in order to bail me out you had to take a note out on the house, would you do it?"

"Depends. How long are you in jail for?"

"Two years."

"What are you in for?"

"Insider trading."

Marti didn't know what that was. It sounded deep, narcotic.

"Think about it," Al said. "There's no right answer."

It wasn't his fault. His siblings used to lay him down in the driveway and steer the family car over him. He wasn't supposed to turn into this kind of man. She wished he had been a bartender, some other honest trade. She would have visited him at work. She would have respected him.

She told the driver where to turn. Right on Grandview, left on Doris Place. It was a windier road at night, more treacherous. She paid and as they walked up the lawn Al held her hand, swinging her arm a little, lifting his nose.

"Smell that?"

Al stopped and raised his foot. It was a big yard, in need of a close mow. The air was dry, swirling.

"Dogshit," he said.

It wasn't. It was deer shit. Marti laughed. James Dean

in Florsheim. That's entertainment.

::

Sundays mornings she watched Charles Kuralt and caught up on correspondence. Al slept in.

The morning light was good when he woke up and looked through the telescope. The Stearns were milling about their living room, harried, as if they were late for church. Al swiveled the scope a few degrees south. He saw firetrucks in the cul-de-sacs. He saw caution tape.

"Is there a block party we weren't invited to?" he yelled to Marti.

At 10 a.m. she turned on the oven. She smelled smoke. It was outside, quietly riding the winds, billowing.

"Al," she said.

It hadn't rained. She wasn't surprised and she wasn't prepared. She picked up the phone.

"911's busy," he said. "I tried."

Through the bay windows she saw her first lick of flame. It was like a crack deal on the street. She stood back, pretending not to watch. She could see tiny figures huddling, darting, overcome. The fire was almost economical, how quickly it moved. She knew that whatever it was, that night on the news broadcasts it would have a name.

Al was in the yard in his seersucker shorts and sandals, with a garden hose. He turned on the Rain Birds full blast.

"I think we can make a stand," he said.

Marti looked up. Fire ran uphill faster than down. There were a hundred homes on the other ridge, at least.

"Everything is made of wood," she said.

His pores were open and she could see his veins, feel his urgency.

"Let's get it in gear," he said.

It could skip them, right over them. It could jump their house like a freeway.

"Go downstairs," he said.

She felt terrible for him. He had just finished the deck, waterproofed the teak.

"What do I grab?"

"As much as you can carry," he said.

She did as she was told. When Hurricane Betsy hit she was the calm one, she didn't panic like her neighbors and buy up all the canned meat and microwave meals. In the room of her inheritance she took whatever looked expensive, jerseys and infielders' mitts and some surgical masks the painters had left behind.

Her arms were full. She heard crackling, smelled tar and shake.

"Where's the Mercedes?"

"You left it in the city."

"We'll take your car," he decided. "Where are the keys?"

"I don't know."

"Where's the Wagner?"

She was confused. It was hot. The fire was making its own wind.

"The Wagner," he said. "You have it?"

She remembered when her father came home cradling an old slip of cardboard he found at a yard sale. "*Say hello to Honus,*" he had told her. There was a crease in it, a fold only perceptible from certain angles, in special light.

"It's worth more than the house," Al said.

She put her mask on. Al declined his. She thought of the Asian women she saw on BART and in line at the pharmacy at Kaiser during flu season, in full-on gas masks.

"What about my things?" she said.

"What things? These *are* your things."

She didn't think it was possible. She thought it was just a game, a sentimental game. A pastime.

"Marti, what things?"

She looked at the pool and batted away the embers in her face that were like fireflies. They could have had pool parties. She could have done laps. Even if it bred mosquitoes.

"Let's go," he said. "We can fight later."

She fought him, flailed. Al couldn't pick her up. He tugged. She felt her socket go. The slope was working against him.

"It's next door," he pleaded. "Why are you doing this!"

She had a surfeit of reasons. She never got a wedding. She had no vows. He never took her to Napa. Children were take it or leave it.

Al's voice was vapor. Marti felt her soles melting. She felt herself heading back inside. Under the bathroom sink she found a sweater she had knit for Avery, a coupon book for kisses Al bought her in '72 and never redeemed, and tangled around it, her necklace with the smaller dream house, the one easier to clean.

She was on all fours. She didn't know who was twirling who. She started to feel faint. She heard an engine start. The windows were shattering, the propane tanks.

Avery, barking at nothing. Gnawing on thorns.

Man of Merritt

Vida Blue and I are on a first name basis. After the second ultrasound we agreed not to name her family names, like Vivien, or Grace. It was not an easy labor. Ainsley was in the last pushes when it happened. Vida Blue's size and the strain: our daughter split Ainsley in two. When she was cremated I commissioned a quilt made out of her clothes, which is still at the dry-cleaners.

She's almost five now, littering the house with little bits of gold foil and sequins. I cut the crusts off her sandwiches. When she cries, she cries in acrylics, glitter running down her face, hiding her face in her sleeves, loud pleading sobs. When she's happy she raises roofs.

She keeps on not brushing her teeth. Her grandparents, Ainsley's parents, will come over unannounced and early on the days I have her. I ask where they are taking my daughter. They say it's none of my business and I won't see her for days.

I know they're loading her up on sugar.

She likes to see the world from my shoulders, as high as she can get. And how can the daddy of a daddy's girl refuse her? She likes what she sees in those rarefied airs.

In four months Vida Blue has grown three inches, and in that time I have grown a fine thick moustache. She is the autobiography of my twenties. She thinks Santa Claus rides around in a zeppelin. I'm morally opposed to raising her organic and gluten-free. She likes tart apples, string cheese. We go on Saturdays to the farmer's market at Lake Merritt. She is the center of attention, cartwheels, haggling for strawberries.

We could go to the one in the Ferry Building, but Vida Blue does not like San Francisco. She is East Bay, through and through. I did not name her Tony Bennett for a reason. It is fun to show Vida Blue how to find her pulse.

::

Ainsley said it was too strong a name to give a girl. She said we couldn't name our daughter after a man. Not just any man, I objected, one of the greatest hurlers of all time … and I opened the numbers book about the Athletics when Vida Blue was called up from Iowa and no-hit the Twins and won the Cy Young and the cover of *Time* in 1971 on a salary of $4,200, shoestring money, the league minimum, before Ainsley was even a glimmer in her litigious parents eyes', and how Finley didn't treat him like the rest of his ballplayers, and how in '73 he won 20 games and the Yankees wanted him and the Reds and he didn't go downhill until he was traded to the Giants. But even then, great God! he hit four homers and nine doubles.

Ainsley didn't know about the blow or the DUI or Blue Moon Odom, mere footnotes.

"Can her middle name at least be Yolo?" she asked.

Vida Yolo Blue it was.

::

Parenting is frozen dinners and arguments about funny bones and guardian angels. Now that Vida Blue's at the age of cognizance and revolt, I hesitate to storm her with anecdotes of her mother, someone she doesn't know, can't see, won't ever know. Sometimes she asks why there are no pictures up of her mother in the house. Her grandparents also wonder why this is. To them it is queer that I haven't enshrined her. It's a chess piece in their custody arsenal.

You see, Ainsley wasn't terribly photogenic.

::

Family law is a deposition joust. There were low-blows, bald lies. Ainsley's parents were pensioners and a spousal unit, intact. I was a single parent without a sitter, on their list of people who should not procreate.

I took out an ad. Two women responded. The first wrote out a long manifesto about her child-care philosophy. It was compelling bullshit and she was forty minutes late to our first play-date. The second, Joan, was more punctual. Vida Blue doesn't need a best friend, I explained, or a mother figure. She is rather easy to please, except when it comes to her breakfast: she doesn't like any brown on her eggs. She likes them runny and scrambled and sometimes poached. Can you do that? Also, if you're not careful, she'll try to boss you around.

People don't just die in childbirth.

::

After six months of attrition, six months of persistence and my not listening, I took Joan's and my lawyer's advice and started dating. I hadn't been with a woman since Ainsley. Joan wanted to set me up with one of her recently divorced friends, Corinne.

"She's not bitter about men?" I wondered.

"She's not nervous *or* bitter," Joan said.

"Because enough years with a person, you forget what's possible between the sexes."

"Trust me, she's not one of those."

Corinne and I saw a flick and went out afterwards for dinner. Her legs weren't bad but she frowned. After a few wines she excused herself to the ladies room, tripping on the carpet in her high heels.

I'm clumsy but I don't break anything. One time I fell down an entire flight of stairs holding a mug of whiskey, and I didn't spill any of it, not a drop. Another time I needed fourteen stitches and severed the nerve to my ring finger, the left one.

"The film." Corinne smelled like hand soap. "Antonioni, is that how you pronounce it? What did you like about it?"

"It wasn't vulgar," I said.

"You can't like something for its negative qualities."

"I married my wife for her negative qualities."

"What happened to her?"

"I can't get into it. She wouldn't get an abortion," I said. "It was childbirth, a lot of medical jargon."

"What is the technical name for it?"

"Vida Yolo Blue," I said.

"That's so sad. That's beautiful. Joan told me you were a stand-up guy. I can see why."

Looking at the wine was making her drunker. I had quit drinking. It was flammable.

"Notice how we don't wear our wedding rings," Corinne said, leaning in. "What was her name again?"

I tried to change the subject to politics or religion. She was hypnotized by the carafe of wine, the house red.

"David," she said.

"Just Dave."

"Not even one glass of cabernet after work? Explain this to me."

Corinne placed her hand on mine. When I withdrew it she looked at me curiously, as if the date had, at any point, gone north. I accused her of working for my in-laws. I felt under her blouse for wires.

When I got home I excused Joan and went down to the wine cellar I built for our second wedding anniversary. The first year is paper and the second year is cotton, or china, and the third is leather. Inside it was heavy air, metallic, mold on the walls. I chose a vintage I knew and sat in our old recliner, where I send Vida Blue when she's disobedient, and poured it vigorously and providently down my gullet. The next evening I poured myself a scotch. I hadn't touched the stuff in three years. Thank God I remembered where Ainsley had hidden it.

::

It's not a question of fitness. Look: Mondays are Vida Blue's chemistry camp and her bagpipe lessons. Tuesdays she learns to walk balancing a book on her head. Joan takes Wednesdays off and Thursdays I furlough my secretaries and when the Giants are in town we walk the Embarcadero and heckle their fans and their stadium that is like a bad restaurant with waiters in baseball uniforms. Vida Blue's grandparents won't honor her schedule. Dining over at their place is like Russian roulette in that you never know if the food poisoning is deliberate. It's not that they can't learn the routine but that they'll change it and do what they did with Ainsley and look where that got us.

They only know the weekend ways to her heart. Vida Blue's not a 3-D or 39 Flavors child. She likes airshows, museums, the largest balls of twine. What I like she likes. She likes sequels and hates Harry Potter, she threw him in the garbage – he wasn't even worth recycling, she said. You would not believe how growing up has changed, how little is expected of her in school, how sports trump arts and even then, it's half-sports with helmets and liability policies, half-fields, halves.

Not so with fatherhood. There is no community of single fathers I know of, maybe there's an association in Alamo or Walnut Creek, but in Lake Merritt there is no one off whom I can bounce my fears or frustrations. There is only Vida Blue, who wakes at 6:30 a.m., clamors for her breakfast of three eggs and a pint of blueberries and rearranges the dining room chairs into a train. I'm up and at 'em for her. I implore her to clean up after herself. If she throws tantrums (she's like her mother in this regard) I will say to her, "Alright, we can't play until your mood improves," and she will sulk for about five minutes, after which she's my best friend once again, and the chalks are strewn all over the floor.

I have an easy time of looking to the long term, of sketching out the trajectory of our lives … and seeing life thusly, as a series of milestones, I absolutely dread giving her 'the talk.'

I'm old fashioned in the sense that the birds and the bees can wait until the third grade.

Maybe Joan will still be around to do it.

Television is a great babysitter, especially the premium

channels. If it's a Friday night I order us boxing on Pay-Per-View. It's educational but her favorite is still *The Princess and the Pirate*. She's one of those who talks during pictures and if someone else is talking she shushes them. There seems to be something about Bob Hope in an eye patch on a desert isle with a treasure map tattooed on his chest that stirs her lady-parts.

"Dave, what is in that trunk?"

"Gold and silver," I said.

"Why are they burying it?" she asked. "Why don't they just deposit it in the bank?"

Her second favorite is the Marx Brothers. *Go West*.

"What did they do when they were shot?" she asked one night.

"Cowboys? They poured whiskey over it," I said.

"No."

"I'll show you."

I mimed blood on my forearm and emptied my pint glass over it.

"See, all better."

Vida Blue was nonplussed.

"Is that what you did when Mom died?"

Grief isn't flammable. It won't catch. I don't have to conceal the fracture from Vida Blue, she can't see it, it's like those Adlibs she loves, you don't know your father shouldn't have a __(noun)__ where his __(verb)__ used to be.

I can't be all that bad, I can still formulate sentences, feed myself. Whatever I have self-diagnosed is wrong … it isn't unlike the time Vida Blue ran a post-route into the ivy and busted her chin open on a sprinkler and probably needed stitches but I sutured it myself because I had watched too many *Love Boats* and DIY shows and allowed our insurance to lapse.

My new drink is Hitachino, an imported beer. Vida Blue knows the Japanese make the best things. She thinks her namesake is a girl.

::

I like Oakland and all, but where are the adults? My neighbors are a gaggle of twentysomethings in corduroy shorts and Jackie Onassis glasses. I seem to be the only parent whose child isn't a fashion statement.

I told Vida Blue for her fourth birthday that I was closing down Lakeshore. I was going to float a bouncy-house on the lake and rent out the Grand Lake Theatre but she was responsible for the invitations. As Joan left that night she stopped me outside Vida Blue's bedroom.

"Listen," she said.

The door was ajar and Vida Blue was writing out the guest list in her karate clothes.

"I'm inviting Esmeralda, yes. And Whit. And, all the single ladies."

Joan nearly fainted laughing. It was better than the Christmas I bought Vida Blue laser tag. She tore open the packaging the morning of and frowned. It was the wrong set, apparently.

"Stupid Santa," she said.

I got it all on camera. The next day the custody verdict came via certified mail.

::

I didn't kidnap Vida Blue but I wanted her to have a good understanding of her country. The best way to see it was by its ballparks. I named them off for her, all 30, not the stadiums but their sponsors.

We Bonnie and Clyde'd it up to Seattle, dodging APBs and Amber Alerts, disguised in liquid tanner. We assumed aliases. She could be anyone she wanted. Safeway Field had a retractable roof. The cops were inept, it was tempting to pull the revolvers out of their holsters. We hitched to Petco and I couldn't identify any of the Padres and we stayed up late at Coronado watching *Some Like it Hot* where Ainsley and I had honeymooned. I told her about Prince Edward and why people call it 'Hotel Del.'

This confused Vida Blue. She thought it was the actual moon we went to.

Our view was of Point Loma, the skies in *Top Gun*. Sea of Cabrillo, Nimitz. The toll booths are empty, the bridges all paid for. It's the early morning when the vulnerabilities are revealed, like galleons lost for centuries suddenly found on radar, right there offshore, all along.

I'm a morning person, even when I wake up in the afternoon. Vida Blue whimpered. It was 6 a.m., sleep in her eyes. On the lam was a game to her.

"Why are we up so early?"

Her mother lived for mornings.

"Pack your things," I said. "It's time for you to go to work."

"I'm tired."

The constant escape. I needed it for my confidence. It was like a month's worth of Prozac.

"You're driving right? Let's see your license."

"Da-ave."

"I forget, do you take your coffee black, or with cream?"

She doesn't want to grow up. We lunched across from Fiscalini Field where when I was her age I saw Griffey Jr. play a week for a team whose mascot, The Bug, was my father's best friend, on the way to Phoenix and Chase Field with the swimming pool in center field, where they let Vida Blue swim so long as she wore inflatable arms.

"I spy …," Vida Blue counted the bleachers, "with my little eye … 46 womans."

Her water wings were deflating. In the shallow end she started a wave.

"One of them looks like your mother."

"Which one?"

I passed her the binoculars. The Orioles had just tied it up. Chlorine and Budweiser.

"Is she mom's sister?"

It was a woman in a Panama hat with – it could have been the magnification – a subjugated expression, as if she was better off at the races, hitting random trifectas, heckling jockeys.

"I don't know," I said. "I haven't seen her toenails yet."

"What color are they?"

"Are we playing twenty questions now?"

We changed costumes. We barnstormed. There were private planes, Cessnas, crop dusters; we were on the no-fly lists. In Tampa I sent her to improv camp, *From Ha to Ha-Ha*. At Arlington the Rangers had consecutive home-stands against the Sox and the Yankees. I enrolled her in a Montessori school during parent-teacher conference week. It was expensive babysitting. Her teacher was also the carpool supervisor. The Thursday game had gone to 12 innings and I was, as Vida Blue reproached me, 'wicked late.'

"She's not speaking up in class," the teacher alerted me.

"Vida Blue talks when she's talked to," I said. "Do you call on her?"

You could tell this woman reined it all in, cold turkey everything, absolute severance from fun.

"It'd be better if you just taught her to raise her hand, like everyone else," she said. "Vida's grade depends on participation."

"Vida Blue doesn't say stupid shit."

"You don't understand," she clarified, "when Vida wants to speak she stands up on her desk."

That's my girl.

::

We caught a one-hitter at Turner Field and her first grand-slam at Kaufman Stadium. Vida Blue pitched here, I said at Fenway. And here, I told her, in the right-field pavilion at Dodger Stadium with the neon wig and lifts to make her look nine years old or ten.

"Is Vida Blue still alive?"

She once asked if I was best friends with Fred Astaire. She is the logic behind adopting dog with the hole in its heart that can't find a home. No point shielding this one from death.

"She is," I said.

"How tall is she?"

I looked up Vida Blue's vitals.

"175 pounds," I said.

"That's tall for a woman," Vida Blue said.

Her mother and I did this very thing on our honeymoon, not this exact route but roads like it, fleet cars, open containers, scenes of crimes and total abandon. It was worth reprising, although I was doing it for myself, and maybe for Vida Blue to one day unpack or scrapbook. I don't think she will block it out or, even worse, remember it wrong, out-of-order. We kept all the ticket stubs and foam fingers, the giveaways and wanted posters. In Santa Fe we stopped for Vida Blue to try on moccasins and to smoke out of Tecumseh's pipe. We toured what used to be Comiskey, Enron Field. A single-A squad in Visalia brawled in front of her and in Asheville she caught her second foul ball.

We drove a Harley through Monument Valley, her helmet two sizes too big. She recognized it from *Stagecoach*. By Cooperstown I was overextended. We tailgated and hitchhiked. There were hard times. We were almost caught in Tuscaloosa in a white Ford Bronco, the joke of which was lost on her. At a Flying J outside Wilmington I explained how people used to travel like this all the time, sleeping in back-seats of stolen cars, under stars.

"Why don't they anymore?"

"Everyone wants to go to Europe," I said.

"That's silly," Vida Blue decided.

We panhandled inside Graceland. At Pecos we recreated the rodeo. These aren't memories, they're prizes. I was, unknowingly, grooming myself. I remembered Jedediah Smith, Al Jolson, the guys on Mt. Rushmore she found so handsome. America's mongrel compost.

It really was silly.

::

Your honor, Vida Blue is growing in ways I can't believe. These days she wants to pay for everything. She has a pink coin purse and won't go anywhere without it.

She doesn't learn about money until the second grade, when she will also learn how to tell time.

If she's good we go up the street after dinner to Fenton's for ice cream.

"How much do I owe you?" she'll ask the clerk in her most adult voice, handing over seventeen cents. "Keep the change!"

Cute kid. I should get her into modeling.

Conversational Braille

Someone from the County was due at his place at 9:30 a.m., sharp. It was the same building Patty Hearst had been kidnapped in, perhaps even the same apartment, Byxbee wasn't certain. He telephoned Nina the day before to confirm. She was his rehab specialist. He had her on speed dial.

"I hope this thug is punctual."

"Mr. Byxbee."

"I want to catch all of batting practice this time."

He could hear her holding the phone away from her ear. All summer Nina had sent him ethnic people working off misdemeanors. Byxbee hoped for a do-gooder this time, an Eagle Scout.

"He's a good kid," Nina said. "Ignacio Valenzuela. Judge said it was the wrong place, wrong friends, too much time on his hands."

"He doesn't have a job?"

"A man and his dreadlocks aren't easily parted."

"How many hours?"

"700," Nina said. "Where's that open mind we talked about?"

The pills for Byxbee's vertigo made him uneven. It was Ménière's. The diagnosis came late. It sounded like one of the grapes blended into champagne. Nina pressed him to try more exotic therapies, acupuncture, aromas. His headaches were migraines, pneumatic drills. He was blind. It all compounded.

"Ignacio?"

"Goes by Nate," Nina said. "He's from the peninsula. We're cousins."

"You're related? That's cheating," Byx said. "I'm easy.

Soup kitchens, those are hard."

"It's not cheating. It's nepotism."

Byxbee hadn't met her, only over the phone. She sounded like she had work done, botox, a pixie cut.

"He's driving in from Daly City," Nina said. "Plus traffic, so be patient. Don't forget your mitt."

He liked her voice, raspy in the mornings. He practiced her open mind exercises, hearing exercises. At her suggestion he chased flies around the house. His touch wasn't as sharp as his intuition or his fear. He drew baths, softened with salts. He used a talking thermometer, his toes. The noises in his apartment were analog voices, co-eds in the stairwell, kegstands upstairs.

::

That evening the cat lady from across the hall, Lyn, helped him paint his cane green with nail varnish. Passing him in the hallway she had offered to help shop for groceries, read bills. It was a miracle he remembered her name. Cal students were year leases, itinerants.

"Byx," Lyn said. "Is the shaft not supposed to be red? It's a foot taller than I am."

Colors were benign to Byx. All he had were equations. Green was Marin, the Shire. Gold was King Tut.

"I don't want anyone mistaking me for an Angels' fan," he said.

He wasn't born with favorites. Growing up in Phoenix he had nothing for the longest time, no Diamondbacks, only Suns. Then he got a dog. He didn't like its name – Avery – or its owner, who hooked the leash to her blouse and bounced around the ceremony convulsing, hysterical. Avery did not adapt to the desert, wasn't cut out for service work. Byx renamed it El Toro, after his favorite pitcher. It shat indoors. It ran.

"I only have one of each. This one's *Emerald Thai Vert*," Lyn said.

"Close enough," Byx said.

"I love painting nails," she said.

He heard her legs uncross, her pants swish. In his year at the California School for the Blind Byx was obliged to dress a certain way, in reflective clothing, name tag, Dickeys. They taught him Braille, domestic sciences. It was three blocks from, of all things, a gentleman's club where he learned more of the world's ways. The girls were close friends, carpooling from Sacramento. They traded off babysitting. "Forgive my blind costume," he told them. He drank Manhattans and they let him touch and complimented his endowment and at closing time poured him into a taxi. Their libidos were surprisingly weak.

"You sound foreign," he told Lyn.

She was Hmong. He was meeting all sorts of people lately. Her cat was stealthy, a Siamese.

"Here Iz. Here." Lyn clicked her tongue. "Maybe she's taking a shit."

"What's your major?"

"Isabel," Lyn called. "She's skittish. She doesn't know how blind you are."

It was her first time living off-campus. Her apartment felt larger than his, more light. Byx felt her shift, prop herself up, light footfalls, purring.

"Like 90 percent, or what?" she asked.

He tried to smile a lot on the street, like it was nothing. He tried to not walk into hydrants. Benvenue was near the Berkeley/Oakland border, a straight shot to campus. The sidewalks were the shoulders of wrestlers, that wide. Byx went down the middle of them, in full view. He was a puddle. People walked around him. It might be urine.

"It's not a measurement," he said.

"I like your sunglasses," Lyn said. "That's what I meant to say."

They were Carerras, the Formula One frames. Byx imagined his empty socket looking gross. He was vain, scared of it and pounds, people grimacing. As he gained weight he started measuring it in stone, kilos. When he threw out his scale he accidentally triggered the sensor. *Ready*, it said in the trash. *Goodbye*.

"Is it a glass eye? Two?" Lyn uncapped the second polish. "This one glitters. *Goldenrod Gingerlily*. I'm like a vice when it comes to secrets. You can tell me."

He did. It was a plastic eye. He was also left-handed.

"I'd be scared to leave the house," Lyn said.

Byx wanted to touch her tits, be in her day-to-day. Homeless people scared her, the broken record of panhandlers. She took the bus to campus, the 30X, reading *US Weekly* on her phone. He could make out shadows of her, outlines. He saw auras. It wasn't all black.

"You have to hate yourself for fifteen minutes," he said. "Then you're ready."

::

"Are you the guy? Byxbee?"

It wasn't a hybrid. Byx heard the engine from blocks away. He doubted it would pass smog.

"You're Nate? Two hours late."

It wasn't his fault. There had been a crash on the Bay Bridge, at the *S* curve.

"Help me in," Byx said.

His cane telescoped. It was not a crutch. He sat up front, shotgun. His sleeve caught in the door.

"You have directions?"

"I can find it," Nate said.

There was impediment in his voice Byx couldn't place, a moustache, missing teeth. The cockpit smelled like incense, old pine cone. Nate's driving was bob and weave. He sped through yellow lights. They were going uphill, Broadway to Hwy 13. Byx leaned into curves.

"These side streets are cute as fuck," Nate said. "Why are you in an Angels hat?"

Byx cringed. He was sensitive to profanity, the nightly news.

"It's the old A's logo. From Kansas City."

"I know George Brett," Nate said.

"You remember that?"

"I *know* him."

"I don't know," Byx said. "Were you even born?"

There were awkward silences. Byx didn't want to nag. He assumed there were cues from Nate he was missing, invitations to make small talk.

"Nina said you don't mind the A's," he said.

The year was special. The team was well over .500. They won in extra innings, walk-off wins. They pied one another.

"Raiders fan," Nate said.

He was terse, omitted prepositions, predicates. He didn't use his blinker.

"Al Davis, that's how you run a team."

"He's got vision," Nate said. "You've been before?"

"For football, no. But I saw David Cone and Roger Clemens," Byx said. "And Jim Abbott when he lost his 16th straight."

He didn't expect accommodations. He wasn't one of those. He wouldn't lawyer up if there wasn't an elevator. The Coliseum was accessible. The sport wasn't.

"Abbott won that game," Nate said, with a savant's assurance.

"You're thinking of another guy," Byx said. "I mean Jim Abbott, the cripple."

"It was his only win that year. It was so long ago," Nate observed. "You probably forgot."

Byx protested, then hedged. Nate could be right. Was.

"I can't believe I fudged it," Byx said.

"It's cool. I was line dancing and doing a full court press on these *chicas* at Saddle Rack and drank myself out of contention and said my uncle was the best ever. Your Abbott is forgiven."

"Your uncle," Byx said.

"I grew up on this shit."

"You grew up on it but you can't find the Coliseum?"

It was a twenty minute ride, door to infield. They had been on the road for half an hour. Nate said he knew a shortcut.

"No, I should thank you for the ride. Really," Byx said. "Nina said she'd take care of the gas. She said you got into some kind of trouble."

Nate downshifted.

"Don't mention it," he said.

The 13 went to Hayward. Byx worried they were in the middle lanes.

"You keep touching your wrist," Nate said. "Nervous?"

Nina had mailed Byx an open-mind gift, one of those *Live Strong* bracelets except with another mantra, in Braille. His fingertips were glossed from years of trolling dots, lightly, as one would a Ouija board. There was a typo in it.

"It's nothing," Byx said. "I don't have HIV."

"Dude," Nate insisted.

It pained Byx. It was patronizing. He was high horse.

"It says '*Positive is how I live.*'"

"Does it work?"

They accelerated. The highway stopped curving. Nate's ankle bracelet beeped. His house arrest had been disabled. Byx felt an exit, a U turn.

"They're moving," Byx said.

"I heard."

"Fremont doesn't want it, but the owners have a hard-on for San Jose."

"South Bay isn't terrible."

"Name one redeeming thing."

"Saddle Rack," Nate said.

As civilians the A's didn't live in San Jose: they rented in Alamo and Clayton in houses next to Jon Gruden's, who (Byx was told) had the same pissed-off look when he was watering his lawn.

"We're close," Nate said.

"Why are we slowing down?"

"You're too statistical," Nate said. "It's a speed trap. I'm Mexican."

Byx also wanted regular treatment. He didn't need help crossing streets. His blindness wasn't his sexuality. It didn't define him.

::

Nate paid $17 to park. It cost more than the tickets combined. "I don't know why we didn't just BART here," he said.

Straily was hurling. It was his second start. They weaved through tailgaters, reggae. Byx listed into a monster truck with ridged wheels. In the tunnel behind home plate he tripped on power cords.

"Forgot my Klonopin," he said. "Fish into water."

It was a park for rookies, small skyboxes. A pitcher's park. Byx pictured fans shuffling like water fowl, ushers who did not smile. The field was below sea level, tarps pulled over the nose-bleeds. They watered the infield between innings. Lyn had read that to him. In the seventh inning they raked it. The visiting team dugout's phone was tapped. There was a point – he couldn't remember – after which no liquor was served. The esplanades were 24-feet wide. He was prepared.

"There was a dog day here in April," Nate said. "One of those promotions where everyone brings dogs. Where's yours?"

Dear Mrs. Breems. His parents had tracked down her address and Brailled the keys on his word processor. *We live on a very busy street. People from Chandler are stupid drivers. Avery was a dog's dog. I don't believe* "All Dogs Go to Heaven" *but I'm sure he did. I really appreciate all your work. Have you seen that movie? They didn't even stop. I'm sorry.*

The letter got returned twice, undeliverable. He buried *El Toro* himself. A cane was less trouble, didn't bark.

"Let's grab some pine," he told Nate.

Their seats were in Section 209, the mezzanine. Across the field, behind the home dugout, Straily's cheering section rattled water bottles filled with coins.

"Put your glove on," Nate said.

Byx felt in his backpack for it. He kneaded the leather, folding it. It needed oiling. The fingers were cool.

"Now what?"

"Catch something," Nate said.

::

Straily struck out the side in the 1st. "All swinging," Nate noted. In the bottom of the inning Coco hit a leadoff single to a groundswell of applause.

"We can't just sit here," Nate said. "Let's do a lap."

Byx took Nate's arm. There was a logjam outside the garlic fries. He walked into a deodorant pocket and needed help finding in the john. It felt decrepit, sulking, old infrastructure. Margaritas were dispensed out of steel boxes in the wall. Beers were eight bucks. He stepped in gum.

"You drove, I'll buy," Byx said.

He used two rubber bands for tens, one for singles. Twenties he paperclipped. He reached into his front pocket. His sleeves shot up. He winced.

"How'd you get these bruises? One Corona, one margarita. I'm double fisting," Nate said. "No, I'm fucking with you. Margarita's yours. Seriously, someone beat you up?"

Byx traced the pain. The bruises were constellations up his forearms, Channel Islands.

"Table your machismo for a minute," he said. "I fell onto the tracks."

"BART?"

"I tried to get on the train. I missed."

"Hold these, will you? You got lucky," Nate said. "Third rail, you're toast."

His condition was what it was. He had to use both hands. Byx tucked his glove under his armpit. He felt feet shuffling, impatience. There were complaints about the Budweiser, the cost.

"You're subsidizing the great play at second base," he said to Nate.

The line grew longer, impatient. It blocked the concourse.

"Nate?"

His tequila was sweet, watered down.

"Nate, you there?"

It spilled. He was crashed into, bumped. He was whirling. He was pinball.

"Fucking wetbacks," Byx said.

Flying blind in public was a daring thing, predicated on trust. He needed handrails, look-outs. If there was anything he hated it was being stranded. His cane was semaphore, an S.O.S.

"Help," he said low, for himself.

It was a day-game. There weren't supposed to be this many people. He felt a hand on his elbow, not a guiding hand but reassuring nonetheless.

"There you are." It was like being rescued at sea. "Where were you?"

Nate took back his Budweiser.

"The wetback hopes you like mustard on your pretzels," Nate said.

"And salt," Byx said. "I didn't mean you."

"I know," Nate said. "Just all Mexicans in general."

::

In the top of the 2nd Straily got Trumbo to pop-out. He had retired four batters in a row. For mid-inning entertainment the mascots with spun around bats and ran the bases. The Macarena skipped over the PA.

They parked themselves in right field. The ushers had departed. They sat where they pleased.

"There's no bad seat here," Byx said.

"They always play good music."

"Nina wouldn't tell me what it is you do," Byx said. "For a living."

"I don't do. I deal."

"Drugs?"

"Pot isn't drugs," Nate said. "It's like playing outfield, you know?"

Byx didn't. It was an unexplained allergy when was two. He never played but he kept score in a ledger, punching E6 and backwards Ks using a slate and stylus. The A's traded their best radio announcers to the Giants. On her off days Lyn lobbed whiffle balls like fungoes in the middle of the street to Byx's outreached glove, landing harmlessly, rolling into gutters.

"You have to trust the grass," Nate said.

That's what Byx loved about baseball. There were no scandals, no religion or sex. Steroids, that was it. Corked bats. Small things.

"Don't look now," Nate said. "You're on the score-board."

"Where?"

"Above left field. On the Megatron. That's us."

Byx straightened. "What did I win?"

"Nothing," Nate said. "Wave."

::

They ate lustily, dogs with sauerkraut, rifling through merchandise, spending without looking. Nina would see they were reimbursed. Mid-inning in the 4th a chain of golf carts snaked through center field, dressed like BART. A drunk in the loge section yelled for a nine-run homer.

In the 5th Nate moved Byx into the bleachers proper, deep in left field. The Angels scored twice. Among the *prolo*, in a drowsy sun, Byx eavesdropped on the minor annoyances, the belching, people who named their daughters after *Twilight*.

"Single Nate?"

"Dating."

"I know this girl in my building," Byx ventured. "Maybe she's your type."

Last night he had wanted to put his lips everywhere, to kiss her tax returns, the backs of her knees. He envied her clever economies, double coupons, Ziplocks on the clothesline. His suavity was unpracticed, wooden.

"It'd be like kissing my brother," Lyn said.

"You don't know until you've tried," Byx said.

She rebuffed him politely. On his way out she used her extra deadbolt.

"Where is this *chica*?" Nate asked.

It was the bottom of the 6th. The A's were down one. Pennington led-off and drew a walk.

"She's cramming for O-Chem," Byx said.

Jemile Weeks grounded out. Crisp doubled. The crowd was agitated, new life. Cliff Pennington scored. Byx clapped his thighs.

"Want to hear some magic?" Nate said.

"Sure."

"What was your first game?"

On five pitches Brandon Moss struck out. Reddick drew a walk.

"It was Finley versus Hershiser," Byx said. "This was the year Percival was lights-out, before Disney bought the *Big A* and put the Matterhorn in center field. I was fifteen. It took seven hours to drive to Anaheim."

Reddick was 'OG.' Cespedes was a 'beast.' What language. On a passed ball Crisp stole third.

"I knew you were an Angels fan," Nate said.

Byx lifted his chin, his mood. Crisp might steal home. They could win the division.

"Classic pitchers' duel. The score's 1-1 into the ninth and they call on Percival --"

Cespedes' bat splintered on a single to center, a ruckus. The A's had the lead again. Byx was being high-fived, hugged.

"And Albert Belle cranks one into center field," Nate

said, ending Byx's sentence. "And after him Jim Thome knocks one into left. Then Sandy Alomar."

The coincidence was unbelievable, impossible. Byx must have mentioned it to Nina. He didn't think she was listening when they talked, taking notes. Things were happening all at once, for once, finally. Byx was taffy, stretched. He was his section's mascot. The Angels were on the ropes. He joined the stomps for Carter, imploring him to blast one into Contra Costa County.

"That was her first game, and mine," Nate said. "Our uncle took us."

"Your uncle again."

"Fernando Valenzuela," Nate said.

El Toro. In baseball, in life there were infinite timeouts. Byx could step out of the box, compose himself. It wasn't basketball. Life was the metaphor.

"I named a dog I hated after your uncle," Byx said.

"You're more of a cat person," Nate said.

"He wouldn't fetch."

"Of course."

"You realize not all blind people want to see," Byx said.

The count was 2-1 on Carter, not necessarily a hitter's count but he would swing anyway, all the stats pointed to it. Byx heard a bag of resin drop to the mound, the pitcher spitting from the stretch, then the sound barrier breaking, a heavy thud, burnt wood.

"Long fly ball," Nate said.

The average home run took four seconds. Byx counted. He couldn't defend himself. They would reach over, spill on him. Knock him over.

"Left field," Nate added.

Someone lifted his right arm. He couldn't feel his bruises, his apprehension. He had practiced for this. He reached.

"It's yours," Nate said.

Byx bent his knees, shaded his eyes. He was the kid in the outfield, the rook, *The Sandlot*.

TWO IOTA

Milo waited in the cafeteria of St. Luke's solo, playing backgammon, waiting for news. The soda machine was broken. His insurance had lapsed. The Jell-o was lime. He was better at chess.

Helen woke up from her sedation asking for cigarettes and about his goats, in that order.

"They want to put Jayne Mansfield out to pasture," Milo said.

Pasture, a euphemism for euthanasia.

"And how's Mata Hari?" she asked.

They were Mytonic goats who, when hit with a stiff wind or an interloper or an errant ball, toppled over in a momentary fit of crowd-pleasing epilepsy. It was a brief somnambula. The fans named them, mostly after movie stars. During games they ran in circles in the petting zoo in right field. Milo talked to them like they were plants. He hemmed at them and bleated. He got attached. They were muscular as terriers and allegedly delicious. His staff was a shillelagh, knotted at the top. There were also sheep.

"She gave birth in the 6th inning," Milo said. "They stopped the game for it."

"Boy or girl?"

"I held it above my head like this," Milo said. "Placenta in my eyes."

"Charles should hire a vet," she said.

Mr. Finley was 'sir' or 'Mr. Finley,' never Charles to his face. Sometimes Chuck.

"He's afraid of the veterinarian-industrial complex," Milo said.

The worst was behind them. When Helen was admitted they didn't know it was meningitis. It was a nurse practitioner in Oncology who diagnosed it, risking her career on a hunch, a conjecture. Doctors were not mechanics but they had missed the flagrant signs, the red spots and fatigue and Helen's intolerance to light. It wasn't one of those ailments like *grippe* that would take her slowly south, Ft. Lauderdale south. She would need months to recuperate. She wouldn't let Milo pity her.

"You'll have to go to the thing without me," she said.

"The thing?"

"The gala."

"I don't know," Milo said.

"No refunds," Helen said. "Your costume idea is brilliant."

It was for a good cause, a ballot measure to keep the Athletics in Kansas City. Finley was courting Oakland. He feted Dallas also, and Louisville. He had that alchemy. The best outfit would win its wearer $1,500, a dizzying sum to Milo.

"There'll be girls there," Helen warned.

"Girls haven't happened to us yet," Milo said.

"Be careful." Her voice oscillated, went limp. "They might fall in love with Jack the Bodice Ripper."

::

Finley kept Milo on payroll as he nursed Helen. It was a week before she was let out of quarantine. When she found out who was paying for her hospitalization, her blood pressure went up forty systolic points.

"Now you're even more indebted," she told Milo.

Three years earlier, during a June day-game against

the Mets, Finley paid a $3,000 incentive to Milo. It was like stumbling upon a duffel bag stuffed with crisp hundreds. He had grown accustomed to grandiose gestures from the boss, from left field as they say, but no gift of Finley's came without strings. Milo had sprinted home to Helen that day, bonus in hand, and in the kitchen he asked her to drop to her knees. It was carpeted.

"With this check," he said, opening his wallet, "I thee wed."

They finally did in 1964, year of Goldwater, of the commercial with the girl plucking the flower and the atom bomb. The engagement had been long, almost perpetual. Helen had stuck by him as he sold swimming pools, wore sandwich boards, a stint in the National Guard. Milo could put away his pride when he needed to, stand in a petting zoo with a shepherd's staff and a Jesus wig, taunted and egged on. Milo didn't tell her about his ulcers, the turnover and the mild attacks he hoped were only nerves, all of which he thought had to do with work, not home. The players could afford to quit. He couldn't.

"We can't take his charity," Helen said.

She was still sick. It was hard for Milo to look at her. She was retaining water. He focused on her unadulterated parts.

"Take it," Milo said.

Her taste buds were gone and she couldn't swallow. She was fed through a tube. She craved curry.

"I'm tired of being poor," she said.

"Hey," Milo said, "what did Bing Crosby say to the bum?"

It was the only yarn of his that had any legs. He felt her forehead. She radiated.

"C'mon, it's funny," he said. *"Prosperity is just around the crooner."*

Helen glistened. It was her body's way of fighting it. She hated the joke. Her vitals were up and down. It was like the cold or flu. Milo forgot what to feed, what to starve. On the day of her discharge she asked Milo to wheel her out.

"I forgot," she said. "You hate ceremony."

Milo had been tending to her bedpans, her soiled gowns.

"It's amazing I made it to our wedding," he said.

It had been a small ceremony, on same day that Khrushchev visited Disneyland.

"You were late," Helen said. "Twenty minutes. That's the bride's job."

City of fountains, city of Charlie Parker. In Westport the ice cream vendors were frequently mugged. On their honeymoon the Athletics' went on a five-game winning streak. Milo returned to work with an inexplicable negativity, sitting out the August downpours, clapping when he had to. During batting practice before every game he painted the A's logo on the best looking of the goats (Rory Calhoun) and the opposing team's colors on the unslightliest (Joan Crawford). The fans were fair-weather people for whom the A's had to win because their happiness that day hinged on it. Milo gave rations of himself away, measured parts. He was Finley's fix-it man, the house detective in charge of the Lost and Found and the Olympic marksman who chalked the foul lines and the welder who bent the foul poles two inches fair. *Frankly speaking,* Finley had written in a commendation, *Milo Duer is the man for the job, no matter what the job actually is.* He looked like one of the Carradine brothers or, when he didn't shave, Dennis Hopper. Kansas City had weakened his constitution. He was made for the clergy, the library, old maid's work.

Milo would never tell Helen this. He was disinclined to open up to anyone, let alone to his wife.

::

Milo dabbled in gambling, never betting against the Athletics although it tempted him to. He sulked when he lost, ashamed at his lack of prophecy. He second-guessed his intuition. He made errors.

"No more of this 'Athletics,'" Finley directed his staff. "We're not in Philly anymore. From now on, it's the A's."

They were episodic in '67, Senators-busting, Braves-busting. By July the season was, mercifully, half-over. Attendance plummeted and the team went with it, as if the two were tethered. Municipal was a necking-park, a first-date park. Its previous names were Muehlbach and Ruppert Parks. In the bullpen the long relievers played left bench, center bench, Skoal. They were on pace to lose 110 games. It was without precedent. Murphy's Law was Finley's Law. The afternoon games were spectacles. Children queued up for Milo's autograph. In the middle of the 3rd the goats were only playing dead but Milo was booed until all of the animals revived. In the 5th he checked out and locked up the zoo and lit up in the equipment room, wearing his rally cap, smoking rally green. Finley, the monument, telephoned in the 7th. Something, everything had invariably gone wrong. Tables were pounded. His voice was coarse, single-ply. It was all Milo's fault. Hands were for fists.

"You're going tonight?" Finley said.

"I am."

Milo had gossiped it to the bat-boy, knowing it would get around to Charles. The old man was slipping but Milo was careful not to make allowances for him on account of his age. Finley had made his money selling insurance with an equation: sweat plus sacrifice equaled success. S was his hourglass, it was linearly independent. Winning was the opposite. It was contingent on the stars.

"What's your gimmick?"

Milo explained it. Finley smelled blood in the water. It was his catnip.

"Corsets," he said. "Who are you, the fucking giveaway king?"

In the 9th as Milo fed the goats (oatmeal cakes on which he snacked on himself, harmless as dog biscuits and as flavorful) a rube from Shawnee in the old A's colors, the blues and the whites, dumped his father's ashes over the left-field fence onto the warning track. Afterward he was removed to the Lost and Found. His name was Reginald. Human remains were a first.

"Reggie," Milo said. "Help me vacuum up your dad and I won't call the coroner."

It had happened at St. Luke's in a ward adjacent to Helen's. Reggie walked in with two short coffees and *croissant* when his father expired.

"He was a season ticket holder," Reginald said. "The doctors were funny. They said I should have gotten larges."

Milo wanted to say Municipal Stadium wasn't a crematorium, but the A's had just lost by seven runs. He stopped himself.

::

Helen had lost twenty pounds and most of her muscle mass. If she hadn't been ill she'd have tried to lose the weight with the heater on in the summer, fasting with her torso layered in saran-wrap. Milo suffered but was supportive. When they were engaged and she announced she was going on a liver cleanse to fit in her mother's wedding dress, he wished her *bon voyage*. She held to it and as a reward he gave her small treats, pastries. "Give me this day my weekly bread," she would say on Sundays. She was a good dieter. Croutons didn't count.

They lived in a duplex near the Pioneer Mother with $5,000 in renter's insurance. Her wedding ring was 18 karat and she had a first-edition of *The Gallery* that could or could not have been signed by John Burns. Milo kept the front lawn fallow so it looked like there was nothing worth vandalizing. If he stood on the couch he could see downtown.

They didn't talk about the side effects. They were thinking wishful. Helen had had a serious bout of it. The damage to her memory was minimal and she tried to conceal it, coughing in the middle of her sentences, holding her hand in front of her face. She was at a loss for words.

"Milo," she called.

He was in the other room, changing. It was 6 p.m. She couldn't find dinner.

His costume – in the catalogue it was referred to as 'The Oliver' – was from a shop in Independence that specialized in historical films and Renaissance Faires. The culottes were a size too big. The shirt had French cuffs, frills. He consulted Helen.

"Am I handsome?"

She was resting on the sofa at an obtuse angle, but

comfortable. She complained about her painkillers. She ate out of straws, now. Milo made a full turn.

"You look like a murderer," she said.

They had met in jury duty. They were the alternates. Her first job was in Charlie Finley's insurance office, one of those secretaries who sat all day but whose feet hurt regardless. She kept a dozen pairs of shoes under her desk, flats, moldy almonds. Her colleagues were not all beautiful; maybe five of the twenty were 10s. Helen Lipp – she had four middle names and was from a long line of people Milo had never heard of. Soon he was in high speed pursuit. On their first date she complained about work and he said he was in her corner and ordered at the bar for her as if he knew what round she would go under. She vowed she would never date a smoker, though she understood how someone like Milo would succumb to peer pressure. She was fond of Finley but baseball confused her, the rules were unclear and she couldn't tell the national anthem from *April in Paris*. Milo cherished her virginity. It was hard being a woman in the sixties, she said – he agreed and said women were islands too, only invulnerable, like Corregidor or Alcatraz, whereas men were indefensible from all sides, like Alameda, Manhattan. He fell deeper, though love to Milo was more like ascension than free-fall. Helen was not entombed. She wasn't thrilled with the neighborhood which was getting "too dark" for her, or with the periphery of their lives, the eclectic friends and furniture, the hand-me-downs and small charities and lesser wines. She let turning thirty get to her. It meant she was not old but irksome. She compartmentalized. There were spaces spouses were supposed to go to, like welterweights to their corners. It pained her that she didn't have a nook to lick her wounds, or the towels she had always associated with married life, eggshell white and monogrammed, his and hers.

Milo sniffed under his arms and at his waist. He got her ice chips. He was not used to polyester, layers of it, or top hats. She was bingeing on the *Lone Ranger*.

"Any front office moves?" she asked.

"Finley re-signed Harrelson," Milo said.

Ken Harrelson, the embodiment of regression. His kryptonite was the change-up. He also chased high heat.

"Ken's the talent," Helen said. "Kiss his ass."

At the stadium Milo fixed everything. At home he only patched things up. He would die in green and gold.

"How late are you staying out?"

"Only for one drink," Milo guessed.

"Famous first words," she said.

He was still handsome, Redford handsome. She didn't like it when he opened beer bottles with his teeth – though his mouth was not in jeopardy – or when waitresses smiled at him. Year-by-year Helen tipped less. She griped at the service. Her water had not been refilled fast enough. Her steak was underdone.

"Are you feeling any better?"

She was not. He put his hand on her forehead. He could live without her. He had thought about it long and hard.

::

The invitation read "fifteen-hundred bones," which Milo took to mean dollars but could very well have been literally that, or another currency. It was at the Star Cuban

on East 18th where, in the name of art or in lieu of it, Bier-
stadts were tomahawked and brassieres embroidered with
American flags burned.

Milo arrived through a lick of dry-ice. He did not take
the signs of the times to heart. There were people dressed as
white whales, roller derby queens, Zorros. In the foyer amid
green-gold streamers a woman was dressed as Dillinger or
Cinderella, Milo couldn't decide. She was built small but
sumptuous, wearing anklets which sparkled, four-inch heels.
She spoke before he had a chance. It was like throwing the
first punch.

"You're staring," the woman said.

"In appreciation."

Milo was wrong. She was Maria from *West Side Story*.
He was way off.

"You look like a good man," she said.

"Depends on the day."

"That's good," she said. "I hope the punchbowl is
spiked. I feel like making some bad decisions tonight."

Her name was Iota. A hundred years ago her dance
card would have been full. She had money and had traveled
to the places where a thumbs-up or *V* sign was an insult, Al-
giers where there were pirates in turbans, Oban and gangs
of dark young men sunning on blinding white beaches. Her
dinners came with instructions. Several of her dresses she
kept locked in a safe.

Milo held out a bodice. He drew it out from under his
cape. She was skeptical.

"What's this?"

"Climb in," he said.

Milo tied her up. He was the bodice ripper but to

his surprise it did not tear. He tugged harder. His fingers weren't working. It was supposed to be no sweat. The draw-strings were tangled. Iota seemed unfazed and told him a little about herself. She had moved to Kansas City from Springfield, the state capital, to "unrepress" herself. Loca-tion mattered, though there were tradeoffs. She hadn't so much as seen a black man, only in National Geographic, until high school when out of an anatomical fascination she squired the half the JV backfield. Thereafter she was ad-dicted to ebony, dreadlocks on her pillow – the urban life over the pastoral – cornrows, not cornfields.

Finally Milo got the corset off.

"There," he said.

"Are you married, Milo?"

"Most nights."

"I would never." Iota shuddered imagining it. "Death, dishes."

It was. It was also Pavlovian. In Milo's duplex there were crucifixes where there had been clocks. On her wom-en's lib papers Helen drew small hearts over her 'I's.

"Shush. Huddle up," Iota said.

"Why?"

"Because I can't do all of this by myself."

In her palm the mushroom lay harmlessly, like shiitake. It took Milo a moment to understand. It was happening in strobe, very fast. She also had 'ludes.

"Come on," she said.

"Just a nibble," Milo agreed.

He expected epiphanies, clarities. Some things didn't translate or they defied explanation. It was brazen, it was telling Hendrix how and when he needed a manicure. Milo's only experimentation with drugs was the occasional Milltown, washed down with Schlitz. Iota salted her neck and offered a shot of Olmeca tequila that she said would accentuate the trip. Milo balked at the chaser and clawed for the worm. He saw rainbows, end to end, *fan*tasmagorias. Iota's shadow was warm. He felt his lucidity d

e

f

l

a

t

i

n

g. In front of a cheese plate he proposed a *fromage de trois*. He was inverting his words, uphill four bottles with two miles of wine. He mangled their order. Time wounds all heals. He wanted water because Iota was two waters in and he wanted her to count his waters and keep the upper hand. He was a jack of all genomes, a healthy man who flushed toilets with his feet. He eavesdropped and stockpiled anecdotes and talked about California – Oakland was new and he could write his name in it like a freshly poured sidewalk – it was honeybees living in the rosemary and hot showers with good pressure and wasps on the windowsill, socked by the steam. He would wake up in Jack London and do the crossword, his mental flex. Finley would let him work 9 to 5 and sometimes 10 to 6. Bruce Lee lived in Oakland. Instead of flowers, which die, he would buy Helen origami magnolias. Black-belt origami – he dropkicked an effigy of Finley. Kansas City was a landlocked, horse-shit town for baseball, Finley had confided to him. The players were not grossly stupid but plain stupid. In the dug-out the method by which an ass was smacked was important. The hand must be convex.

He demonstrated it on Iota.

"I see why he's fired you twice," she said.

"Yes, first I asked for a raise, then a desk. Mr. Finley's very earnest," Milo said. "As in, the importance of being."

"He's got your goat."

"I forgot to feed them," Milo remembered. Earlier he had left the stadium in a hurry.

"Oh, shit," he said.

"Not now. Zoos are depressing," Iota said.

He couldn't drive in his condition. It felt like X's were drawn over his eyes. Outside a tandem bicycle was parked, resting against a No Parking sign without a lock. It didn't matter whose. Milo said a few hasty goodbyes, mounting it like a horse.

Iota preferred beach cruisers, the one speed. She offered to steer. It mattered to Milo that she could *ride*, whereas Helen had never learned. In Amsterdam she had tried and crashed. She hadn't climaxed on that trip; even before her illness it had been months since she had. She was hyper-monogamous. There was a lot Helen couldn't do.

::

It was half a mile to Municipal, downhill, vertiginous. Iota loved his costume; she was a kindergarten teacher with her praise. They coasted and debated current events, the Suez Canal, Cher. Iota had not warned Milo of how good he would feel, how he would come to regret having taken such a small dose because the high wasn't sustainable. He tried to block out time. He counted to ten: a, b, 3 … It felt like the clocks just went forward, and in the morning he would return to his small life, cheated of time. He looked at his watch: it had five arms. It made total sense.

At Municipal one parked in the Satchel Paige section, or under a picture of Campy Campaneris. Milo had the master keys, the skeletons, affixed to a caribiner on his belt-loop. The outfield walls were cavernous, deceptively deep. Sprinklers tore ACLs, ended careers. The infield was quick-sand and behind home plate was a mechanical rabbit which fed fresh baseballs to the umpires.

It was like breaking into what used to be a bank. The vaults were empty but one could imagine the old riches, the passionate fans, double plays as smoothly turned as choreography.

Iota stood on top of the home dugout. She mimed a homer and ran the bases, clockwise, giggling. Milo opened the pen. She tripped passing third. As she rounded first Milo's humor left him.

"Come introduce yourself," he said.

The goats were not his but they were interchangeable with his goals. In a commotion the goats stampeded and grazed in right field. They wore bells, name tags. Their pupils were oval. They were fertilizer. The sheep were in among them, the mules.

"Goats," Iota called. "Come here, you fuckers."

She sprinted at them, clapped her thighs, talked their language, baa! Her voice was a bullhorn, her dress was over her head, Milo began to spin, baa! Baa! Baa! Baa! Baa! Baa! Baa! Baa! Baa! Baa! Baa! Baa! Baa! Baa! Baa! Baa! Baa! Baa! Baa! Baa! Baa! Baa! Baa! Baa! Baa! Baa! Baa! Baa!

Baa! Baa! Baa! Baa! Baa! Baa! Baa! Baa! Baa! Baa! Baa!
Baa! Baa! Baa! Baa! Baa! Baa! Baa! Baa! Baa! Baa! Baa!
Baa! Baa! Baa! Baa! Baa! Baa! Baa! Baa! Baa! Baa! Baa!
Baa! Baa! Baa! Baa! Baa! Baa! Baa! Baa! Baa! Baa! Baa!
Baa! Baa! Baa! Baa! Baa! Baa! Baa! Baa! Baa! Baa! Baa!
Baa! Baa! Baa! Baa! Baa! Baa! Baa! Baa! Baa! Baa! Baa!
Baa! Baa! Baa! Baa! Baa! Baa! Baa! Baa! Baa! Baa! Baa!
Baa! Baa! Baa! Baa! Baa! Baa! Baa! Baa! Baa! Baa! Baa!
Baa! Baa! Baa! Baa! Baa! Baa! Baa! Baa! Baa! Baa! Baa!
Baa! Baa! Baa! Baa! Baa! Baa! Baa! Baa! Baa! Baa! Baa!
Baa! Baa! Baa! Baa! Baa! Baa! Baa! Baa! Baa! Baa! Baa!
Baa! Baa! Baa! Baa! Baa! Baa! Baa! Baa! Baa! Baa! Baa!
Baa! Baa! Baa! Baa! Baa! Baa! Baa! Baa! Baa! Baa! Baa!
Baa! Baa! Baa! Baa! Baa! Baa! Baa! Baa! Baa! Baa! Baa!
Baa! Baa! Baa! Baa! Baa! Baa! Baa! Baa! Baa! Baa! Baa!
Baa! Baa! Baa! Baa! Baa! Baa! Baa! Baa! Baa! Baa! Baa!
Baa! Baa! Baa! Baa! Baa! Baa! Baa! Baa! Baa! Baa! Baa!
Baa! Baa! Baa! Baa! Baa! Baa! Baa! Baa! Baa! Baa! Baa!
Baa! Baa! Baa! Baa! Baa! Baa! Baa! Baa! Baa! Baa! Baa!
Baa! Baa! Baa! Baa! Baa! Baa! Baa! Baa! Baa! Baa! Baa!
Baa! Baa! Baa! Baa! Baa! Baa! Baa! Baa! Baa! Baa! Baa!
Baa! Baa! Baa! Baa! Baa! Baa! Baa! Baa! Baa! Baa! Baa!
Baa! Baa! Baa! Baa! Baa! Baa! Baa! Baa! Baa! Baa! Baa!
Baa! Baa! Baa! Baa! Baa! Baa! Baa! Baa! Baa! Baa! Baa!
Baa! Baa! Baa! Baa! Baa! Baa! Baa! Baa! Baa! Baa! Baa!
Baa! Baa! Baa! Baa! Baa! Baa! Baa! Baa! Baa! Baa! Baa!
Baa! Baa! Baa! Baa! Baa! Baa! Baa! Baa! Baa! Baa! Baa!
Baa! Baa! Baa! Baa! Baa! Baa! Baa! Baa! Baa! Baa! Baa!
Baa! Baa! Baa! Baa! Baa! Baa! Baa! Baa! Baa! Baa! Baa!
Baa! Baa! Baa! Baa! Baa! Baa! Baa! Baa! Baa! Baa! Baa!
Baa! Baa! Baa! Baa! Baa! Baa! Baa! Baa! Baa! Baa! Baa!

Baa! Baa! Baa! Baa! Baa! Baa! Baa! Baa! Baa! Baa! Baa!
Baa! Baa! Baa! Baa! Baa! Baa! Baa! Baa! Baa! Baa! Baa!
Baa! Baa! Baa! Baa! Baa! Baa! Baa! Baa! Baa! Baa! Baa!
Baa! Baa! Baa! Baa! Baa! Baa! Baa! Baa! Baa! Baa! Baa!
Baa! Baa! Baa! Baa! Baa! Baa! Baa! Baa! Baa! Baa! Baa!
Baa! Baa! Baa! Baa! Baa! Baa! Baa! Baa! Baa! Baa! Baa!
Baa! Baa! Baa! Baa! Baa! Baa! Baa! Baa! Baa! Baa! Baa!
Baa! Baa! Baa! Baa! Baa! Baa! Baa! Baa! Baa! Baa! Baa!
Baa! Baa! Baa! Baa! Baa! Baa! Baa! Baa! Baa! Baa! Baa!
Baa! Baa! Baa! Baa! Baa! Baa! Baa! Baa! Baa! Baa! Baa!
Baa! Baa! Baa! Baa! Baa! Baa! Baa! Baa! Baa! Baa! Baa!
Baa! Baa! Baa! Baa! Baa! Baa! Baa! Baa! Baa! Baa! Baa!
Baa! Baa! Baa! Baa! Baa! Baa! Baa! Baa! Baa! Baa! Baa!
Baa! Baa! Baa! Baa! Baa! Baa! Baa! Baa! Baa! Baa! Baa!
Baa! Baa! Baa! Baa! Baa! Baa! Baa! Baa! Baa! Baa! Baa!
Baa! Baa! Baa! Baa! Baa! Baa! Baa! Baa! Baa! Baa! Baa!
Baa! Baa! Baa! Baa! Baa! Baa! Baa! Baa! Baa! Baa! Baa!
Baa! Baa! Baa! Baa! Baa! Baa! Baa! Baa! Baa! Baa! Baa!
Baa! Baa! Baa! Baa! Baa! Baa! Baa! Baa! Baa! Baa! Baa!
Baa! Baa! Baa! Baa! Baa! Baa! Baa! Baa! Baa! Baa! Baa!
Baa! Baa! Baa! Baa! Baa! Baa! Baa! Baa! Baa! Baa! Baa!
Baa! Baa! Baa! Baa! Baa! Baa! Baa! Baa! Baa! Baa! Baa!
Baa! Baa! Baa! Baa! Baa! Baa! Baa! Baa! Baa! Baa! Baa!
Baa! Baa! Baa! Baa! Baa! Baa! Baa! Baa! Baa! Baa! Baa!
Baa! Baa! Baa! Baa! Baa! Baa! Baa! Baa! Baa! Baa! Baa!
Baa! Baa! Baa! Baa! Baa! Baa! Baa! Baa! Baa! Baa! Baa!
Baa! Baa! Baa! Baa! Baa! Baa! Baa! Baa! Baa! Baa! Baa!
Baa! Baa! Baa! Baa! Baa! Baa! Baa! Baa! Baa! Baa! Baa!
Baa! Baa! Baa! Baa! Baa! Baa! Baa! Baa! Baa! Baa! Baa!
Baa! Baa! Baa! Baa! Baa! Baa! Baa! Baa! Baa! Baa! Baa!

Baa! Baa! Baa! Baa! Baa! Baa! Baa! Baa! Baa! Baa! Baa!
Baa! Baa! Baa! Baa! Baa! Baa! Baa! Baa! Baa! Baa! Baa!
Baa! Baa! Baa! Baa! Baa! Baa! Baa! Baa! Baa! Baa! Baa!
Baa! Baa! Baa! Baa! Baa! Baa! Baa! Baa! Baa! Baa! Baa!
Baa! Baa! Baa! Baa! Baa! Baa! Baa! Baa! Baa! Baa! Baa!
Baa! Baa! Baa! Baa! Baa! Baa! Baa! Baa! Baa! Baa! Baa!
Baa! Baa! Baa! Baa! Baa! Baa! Baa! Baa! Baa! Baa! Baa!
Baa! Baa! Baa! Baa! Baa! Baa! Baa! Baa! Baa! Baa! Baa!
Baa! Baa! Baa! Baa! Baa! Baa! Baa! Baa! Baa! Baa! Baa!
Baa! Baa! Baa! Baa! Baa! Baa! Baa! Baa! Baa! Baa! Baa!
Baa! Baa! Baa! Baa! Baa! Baa! Baa! Baa! Baa! Baa! Baa!
Baa! Baa! Baa! Baa! Baa! Baa! Baa! Baa! Baa! Baa! Baa!
Baa! Baa! Baa! Baa! Baa! Baa! Baa! Baa! Baa! Baa! Baa!
Baa! Baa! Baa! Baa! Baa! Baa! Baa! Baa! Baa! Baa! Baa!
Baa!

Conspiracies were not always elaborate. The herd was
dead like always – they had toppled formulaically, it wasn't
that they were trained but bred this way – but not redoubt-
able like always. Milo's eyes were wool, a mirage. He im-
plored for them to wake, to rise.

"You're the devil," he told Iota, gesturing to her, no
nurse, for a stethoscope, a pulse.

The sheep were playing tricks on him, the goats were
in league, baa! It would go on his record, like *Semper Fidelis*
on a dishonorably discharged Marine. He was a child again,
crying before he was beaten, crying into carburetors, wiping
his eyes on windows, calamity.

He pressed on their chests. He dreamed of their knotted, disjointed rising, their delectable milk, tender entreaties
for feed.

Iota had scared them to death. They were in that sleep

which is great. Milo held his breath. He was saving it for his apology to Finley, to Helen – an intricate, serpentine sorry for himself.

PARALLEL FIFTHS

In her CapuCinema tote Yolo packed ballet flats, sarongs and a toothbrush long enough to gag on. She was celebrating *Phospenes' Aurals*, Gaucho's thirty-first blockbuster, a big-budget intrigue with a little something for everyone.

It was luggage she could run with, if need be. There were spiders on Tortola but no snakes. The timeshare, Marienbad, on stilts and setback forty feet from the Gulf, had been advertised to Yolo as

A Gentleman's Imperatives Incubated
Travel | Voyeurism | Winning

She had been advised against fraternizing with its *lowercaste* patrons, the island hoppers and snowbirds dozing in the mildewed rattan, placidly waiting out the travel embargo with her.

Yolo made do. In the harbor of Long Look were fiberglass ships, trimarans racing around buoys, tacking for wind. Ashore it was a skin world of exotic fruits, bootleg virility drinks. She water-skied and nursed virgin daiquiris rimmed with orchids which she stacked behind her ears. She pacified herself with sugars, spending her health and her *carte blanche* on room service that was swift as sorghum. Marienbad cuisine was three fusions, a case (from Yolo's discriminating palate) of too many kitchens in the cook. There were other farcical efficiencies. Earth accommodated the billions, but it had stopped mothering. The deserts were solar landscapes; foie gras was humane again. Man had not yet found a substitute for food.

On hardwood floors as worn as Skeeball lanes she learned old fashioned steps, line-dancing, the Charleston, in exercise gear she cobbled together from the gift shop, shorts with *I Heart BVI* emblazoned on the cheeks. Tanning under the six-meter diving platforms, she consulted her Frommer's. Caribbean history was sunstroke and dengue, rum and civilization, in that order. When she wasn't poolside she was enmeshed in netting, folding origami magnolias, impulse buys of *fromages*-of-the-month and a subscription to Padded Cell – her cousin, Daughn, was committed there – which marketed airtime with its inmates as 'Pen Pals Without the Paper Trail.'

She selected the 'Uncensored Brainstorm' package, a bargain at 65£. It financed upgrades to the sanitarium, stronger electroshock, training videos in lieu of *One Who Flew Over the Cookoo's Nest.*

"Cuz," Yolo said. "Who were you today?"

It had been months since she had seen Daughn, which seemed to her slower than other time, let alone heard from him.

"I'm rarely roses," he replied. The operators were listening in. "I'm never gold bars."

Daughn was himself for once. Her fortune was in spades. Most days he was a plural of obsolete men, game show hosts, encyclopedia salesmen. He was the most lucid in his ward and invaluable in the laundry. He could fold.

Yolo hyperbolized her family history. At age 2 she did not cry much, she liked bread and slept soundly in dresser-drawers while Daughn – a colloquial name, a national anthem name, *by the Daughn's early light* – took to spoiling his bed, dissociating, talking in what his parents first thought were tongues. What remained of Oakland in those days, before the diaspora, was unrest, potholes and cloverleaves, landmarks such as the Mormon Tabernacle in need of razing. It was hard to accept *Raider Nation, CA*, as her revised birthplace, the naming rights exchanged for a bailout, silver and black on all correspondence. The A's had left and her formative years were all about finding the right chunks of asphalt to throw at the cops – a tomboyish, heartfelt dissent against forces which were doing her incalculable good. In protest she traipsed up the port cranes that inspired the sub-par space films and tramped about in Fredrick Law Olmstead's cemetery as they exhumed the graves, gleaning from the Mexicans operating the Bobcats on how to roll her *R*s, as if she knew she would have to *prrrr* to get ahead.

To get even. It was what started her studying motion pictures. She caught up on her Capra, her Truffaut, blossoming into feminism and spreading her legs, not abusing the system so much as exploiting her privilege. At Capu-Cinema, the stable of *de facto* actors, she had been hired on as an institutional memory, a repository of generally useless histories. She was ambitious, but to stand the industry on its head Yolo first required a grip of its feet. In dense memoranda she advocated for renovation of the Rialtos and Lidos, theatres with plush seats and double features and attendants in the loos.

Yolo's life had not been worth much as herself. She had always wanted to be someone else – it ran in the family. When she was assigned to Gaucho it was not a miracle but random selection and her discreet promiscuity paying off. Gaucho was more efficient than a flesh actor, no acting coaches or lost motivations. He couldn't OD.

Learning Gaucho was like learning piano, graduating from *Chopsticks* to *Sail Away*, then Chopin. Yolo was shorthanded, working at 1.5 FTE. Stings and barbs were the price of foliage; she plowed through and tuned out her colleagues' ire, a self-preservation they interpreted as apathy. In spare moments to herself – small times she had to piece together as if by collage – she waited for something electric to fall on her, lightning, unmarried men.

"You won't believe it. Staying, in this resort," Yolo told Daughn. "A *the*spian."

Her lisp was fraudulent. For days she had spied on him, Wallis, grotesque enough for niche acting parts, out filming nothing with a Rolleiflex that customs had failed to confiscate, meditating furiously at low tide and snorkeling in the fetid estuaries. His Gaucho Quotient appeared nil. He seemed to not know. Bodies of water were to look at, not for swimming.

"There's a Persian girl here," Daughn said. "Not worth *fatwah*ing over, but Gaucho would. He just doesn't add up. *Halcyon* was made in '15. Gaucho was 21 then. It's 2027 now and he's listed as 25."

From holes in the PVC rimming the *cabanas* was pumped cool, cannabis-scented mist. Yolo stiffened her voice to parry. Her allotted time with Daughn was dwindling. Women mailed Gaucho kisses, parts of themselves screened for explosives, as if the logic of him was that of a long-distance romance. At CapuCinema it was rumored Yolo was on an early menopause because she didn't brag about her casual lovers, the locally spawned ballplayers she trusted because they offered themselves so freely – seductions executed deftly, as if it was their idea, all along. The parameters of obscurantism had expanded because of Gaucho, but men remained cattle. They consumed what they were fed.

"We're aging him too quickly," she replied.

It was also the logic of monuments. Gaucho was immortal in his animation, his animus. The singularity much ballyhooed in the beginning of the century never materialized. 2027 was the future, or it was post-history. God was dead again, this time for good. Man was getting back to basics. Inheritances were diverted to the state, churches were converted into condos. At Wimbledon the tennis pros wore black.

::

"The trouble with 'every man for himself,'" Gaucho was quoted in *Vi-Che*, "is that the mantra morphs into many men only about themselves, anarchies and archetypes of testosterone where like Huns they pillage heifers in singles and cougars' clubs."

Yolo had not written or deployed this. She was in charge of Gaucho's tabloid life, easing him back into the public's good graces after the DUIs she orchestrated, the manslaughters. It was the circumvention she always anticipated, though there were safeguards she thought were impossible to breach. After his *Vi-Che* interview hundreds wrote in with death threats. His best fans pointed out the customary typos.

It would boil over, Yolo was sure. Her Marienbad regimens were not physical – she was not clockwork like Immanuel Kant's constitutionals or forever like Gaucho's five-o-clock shadow. Time flew miles at a time. Her measure of it was not a timepiece but an odometer in the console of a Swedish automobile, a relic with fueling instructions that were pictures instead of words. On the roads of Tortola she could make protected lefts – wildlife had the right-of-way – and on her aimless sorties she discovered anomalies of gravity where her automobile rolled backwards and up-hill, simultaneously. Only the unpublished resort amenities amused her, the lawn bowling and collaborative massage: the others were synonymous with leisure but they weren't tailored to her: she couldn't all of a sudden just *golf*.

She was unfazed. She held fast to her inertia; she gained. The gymnasium was one of those things one did on vacation – or did not – not because it was vogue but because it could be vogue, might be vogue, or long enough ago, was. It was an unlikely venue for Wallis to accost her, before her buffet hour. Resort encounters were supposed to be inconsequential. Yolo was skimming through a relic she picked up in the resort library, fourth on the waiting list for the ellipticals submerged in placenta-infused pools, a treatment purported to improve her skin, that infernal organ.

He didn't introduce himself as much as crank up his camera and enumerate his favorite botanicals.

"*Pinnatifida, cynara,* they're great for your heart," Wallis asserted, "and by that I mean the actual muscle."

He was rapid-fire inquisitive, a smile like the tip of the cap, foppish and endearing. Who was she? Did she have any pets? After a few minutes Wallis was like Liberace and Yolo's keys were tickled, piqued. What was her industry?

"I background Gaucho," she said. "I'm his obbligato."

She was accustomed to concessions, *quid pro quos*, but she had to bleed it out of him: how he had eloped into a troupe and took up acting not as a vocation but a profession, as if there was money in it. As Wallis described the life Yolo recalled that she herself had never looked or leapt. Did she know it, he inquired, *that* life, sleeping on couches, stenciling trash-cans, *real* life, what did she know? He fanned out his notices, write-ups of him in defunct newspapers. In a revival of *The Coward* he was too shrill. In *Champion* he dropped his lines, when all he had to do was punch. He had to cut his teeth somehow: all the repertories, where they had once taught the essence of acting instead of the nuts and bolts, were shuttered. It was enough for anachronisms alone to elevate characters, not certifications. Besides, the schools had only existed, as one administrator had put it, to provide sex for students, cheap revivals for alumni, and parking for faculty.

"You're whirring," Yolo observed.

She had seen Rolleiflexes in the CapuCinema vault, inferior to Revere Eights but more portable than, say, a Bell and Howell.

"I never part with it," Wallis said, squaring her up in his viewfinder. "The camera hates you."

"It loves Gaucho. Don't you need a permit for this?"

"There's also no script. We're winging it."

Tortola offered him a cheap talent pool, locals clamoring to play as extras. He shot hours of coverage. There was nothing else to do.

"I'd wish you luck," Yolo said, "but I'd rather you broke a leg."

She had stayed out of it, the slapdash production schedule, period costuming and arbitrary cuts. It was a novice effort, an artists' project, a working title. In weaker moments when her curiosity bested her she eavesdropped on the resort scuttlebutt to get an idea of it. Conversation supplanted action, was the rumor. If it sinned it sinned toward excess.

"I keep saying 'it.' 'It' has a name, of course. *First Year at Marienbad.* Clever, isn't it?"

Yolo nodded.

"Because," he said, "you know we're never leaving this island."

His *Marienbad* was, like its namesake, a many mirrored hall of mirrors, a grotesquerie, a laceration of the canon. Wallis was uninjured by stereotypes, aloof to stigma. It offended him that Gaucho bogarted the terrain of film, just as oral rinses supplanted dentists and oral largely replaced kissing. Yolo tried not to pity him. He was nothing like her father, who cursed Mt. Diablo because it made him feel inconsequential, whose happiness and Oakland's successes were inextricably linked, who did not kidnap her as much as take her on an extended detour, who taught her that every strikeout was an elegy, who said that a knowledge of sports meant she could liken all of life's curveballs to a boxing match. Her family tree was an incestuous, athletic cartography of California. She had wanted to be many things as a girl, but royalty never materialized, and modeling meant no *croissant.* No matter: not all lives were equal and it was fruitless dredging up memories, debating alienable trivialities with Wallis, such as his likelihood to diva-up in his trailer, turn fat, cry off-cue, or his rights to free speech.

"Actors went extinct," Yolo said, "because actors became politicians."

"John Wayne using BART, cheering on Reggie Jackson, being human, lung cancer. Is that so hard to imagine?"

"They shouldn't be amongst us, mingling. It's like the critic Koestenbaum says, 'Lives are ruined by nearness to stars.'"

"At least we have Koestenbaum in common," Wallis said. "He also said most events in life are insufficiently sexual."

Yolo didn't disagree. Wallis capitalized and invited her to the hotel bar occupying Marienbad's upper floors.

It pleased Yolo. She dominated rooftops.

"You work for *fakirs* like Gaucho, pixilations. I want to cure your aversion to people," Wallis said.

He was operating on her by attrition. Yolo felt her resistance unravel.

"I'm thirty-two," she disclosed, "old maid's territory, legs for radio," omitting that she was also finicky about her espresso.

"It'll be like those old gin commercials." Wallis offered Yolo a chivalry – his arm. "We'll seize the night by the *Juniperus*."

::

"In every way, I *am* time," Gaucho told *Spoke*, a scandal-sheet second only in circulation to *Spy*. "Lifespans are now at 150, the final 100 years of which isn't useful. Take the civil servants whose pensions vest at 92. I'll never have to trudge like they do. Septuagenarian stew, trudge. Octogenarian offal."

The manipulation of Gaucho – at root he was just a sequence of 1s and 0s, sonnets of source code – or rather the circumvention of Yolo, as it came to be known, approached its nadir. It spawned the end of her teetotaling. *Uppercaste* ingénues were jammed into Watering Hole, Marienbad's 43rd floor bar, a berth of fifths and magnums ensconced in a half-

formed hexagonal neon egg, staffed by bartendresses painted like geishas. There were unstated dress codes throughout
Tortola, which for Yolo was akin to parochial school *redux*:
no skirts above the knee, no legs. The girls were amoricides:
designers trying to make it big, passionate defenders of
sweatshops. Yolo had only a Rosetta Stone knowledge of
this generation, of schizophrenics like Daughn and the new
Oakland, where she was alone in a four-plex in the basin
that was Lake Merritt before it was drained, solitary with
her fetishes, her cutlery and the succulents with whom she
got along well but without any chemistry, because she watered them. Her kitchen was narrow yet serviceable. It was
just her. No one to bump into, or scald.

"It's a calm life, Gaucho notwithstanding," she told
Wallis, knotting the brandied cherry stems with her tongue,
her party trick. "Fairly ho-hum."

He wasn't single, he was between women. She had on
her Sacagawea dress, down to her anklet, no slip or makeup.
She intended to make it easy for Wallis. He would not have
to court her into submission. Lipstick was to write with, not
wear.

"Ho-hum people don't do car bombs," Wallis said.

His trick was reciting the Gettysburg Address. He was
also a Shakespeare-denier. At his urging she volunteered
information about Gaucho, trade secrets, surrendering her
copyrights simply by saying them out aloud. Working on the
inside took the thrill out of celebrity gossip, but there were
compensations: in a spreadsheet she kept computations of
how much she could sell Gaucho's secrets for, which like a
dam she slowly leaked out.

"How much?"

"It's Monopoly money," she said.

There was no model for Gaucho – none living – but Yolo consulted her idols at times, the Glenn Fords and Ramon Novarros she would have taken as her lovers in the bygone era of swing and celluloid and wire-hanger abortions. The sacredness of virginity in the years since had been linked to one's age and then to the breakage itself, the human aversion to pre-possession, i.e. used goods. Hopefully Wallis was not the jealous type, intimidated by her knowledge of men.

He motioned for a third libation.

"Please don't," Yolo said. "I was going to already. I want you to remember some of it."

There were those she couldn't touch and others she couldn't stop touching. Wallis was a gentleman when she fell two garments behind during strip poker in his cabana, the doors to which were teak and warping. The fundamentals of seduction had not changed. Corseted in uncharitable mirrors on the ceiling, she took a few minutes alone to hyperventilate before she deified Wallis, aware of his clandestine filming, bruising her kneecaps, nothing like the parabola of cinema where the climax was the crest of the love story. She detailed his imperfections, the faint shit-streaks in his briefs, his skin tags and eczema on his elbows. Wallis called into question Gaucho's existence, not the fact of him on marquees but his and Yolo's staunch objection to flesh. He gouged her, as Koestenbaum so famously phrased it, to prove he posed no impediment. He wanted a name in the topmost echelons, a name with panache and square footage that he could do honor to and eventually shame.

Thoughts of home crept in – home, an expression

which like 'Mom and Pop' was bad for business. When she swallowed Wallis lip-synced his thanks and invoked the Lord, a breach of the universal etiquette. He wasn't supposed to know such language, not out loud.

::

"If we all lost just 5 kilos," Gaucho told *Spy*, "the world might spin faster."

The tabloids, a cartel of rumor mills in league with CapuCinema, outed Yolo, severing her from Gaucho. Wallis reveled in the maelstrom, outlandishly behaving, opening umbrellas indoors and hurling expletives at mothers who were nursing.

He had been born on a Friday the 13th, he explained. He was safe from superstition.

Tortola's commerces were simple and manualized: free-diving for shellfish, cockfighting. Wallis filmed Yolo in the acreages of papaya, which flourished for centuries in dense outcroppings on the perimeter of Marienbad and were still harvested by hand. Yolo was not a machine although she envied them. They were reliable and in a way so was Wallis: his cockeyed manner as he towed her chapeau, its undulating crinoline brim, directing her and trespassing where the caution tape had gone limp.

He lacked permissions but not gumptions. He was shaking her faith, not circuitously but head-on. It was not her first melodrama but her first in an exotic locale, Tiki bars excepted. Marienbad was a prism Yolo couldn't pass through without deflection. She had shed her exoskeleton, her thoroughly lived and hard-boiled self. She was finding strides she once thought lost. With a soprano ukulele he sang to her,

> *I'll be your Alysheba*
> *You'll be my Alydar*

who, Wallis explained, were not unrequited Arabian lovers but horses.

"I don't know why I sing, I really shouldn't. Alydar lost in photos," he clarified, "by noses," in the likely event Yolo didn't know: some species were constant bridesmaids.

::

Yolo was jettisoning cubes of ice into rancid muscatel when the resort staff walked out, polite and single-file, down to the valets and the craps dealers. They sought unionization, profit-sharing, political asylums not usually extended to the *middlecaste*. She was about to petition for scabs when Marienbad's guests began to pick up the slack, folding napkins in the commissary, janitorial, wreathing the mezzanine balustrades in advance of the premiere screening of *First Year*, laying down ropes and fistfuls of tinsel in what had been the wedding chapel.

Yolo queued up in front of Wallis. It was no big deal, nothing like Gaucho's opening night releases at the Paramount, where she was seated front and center next to his hologram, and the compulsory applause lasted for what seemed like decades.

The chapel was jam-packed, ascots and other raiment. Yolo felt a hand on the small of her back, where she was tattooed with a silhouette of Chaplin as *The Tramp*.

"Don't," she said. "I'm ticklish."

She had Kubrick on the brain.

"I'm trying to get you off," Wallis said.

The Tramp was her hair trigger.

"Off," he repeated. "The red carpet isn't for you."

"I'm sorry?"

"This is mine," he said. "Go around."

Yolo's taste buds burst. He had no clue who she once was. The *ur*-woman. Her name used to stand for something.

"Let go. I'll break your nails," Wallis warned.

Gaucho was eroding. It cited the days she had spent extricating herself from sundry miseries, such as the afternoon at 17 when everything she had learned about …

"She's bucking."

… calculus evaporated, all the rules and cosigns; the night Daughn melted down, lost for three days in the Muir Woods, stumbling upon mysteries she only later came to understand …

"Drag her out by her hair."

… and the afternoon she tried to swim off of Tortola, jaded by cicadas. A trawler had rescued her on an artificial reef a mile out, her lips cratered, Mako sharks stalking.

Yolo tripped over the velvet ropes. Her dress had shredded. One of her molars was missing.

"You might as well have just slit your wrists," Wallis said.

The chapel concurred, impatient for the credits. Yolo stumbled and slammed the revolving doors, chaotic in the bonsai gardens, clutching lampposts along the resort paths, hanging on by the skin of her skin. As she trashed her cabana Yolo vowed to herself that she would start a food series, *Salads of Shock and Awe*, after her mastectomies. She would become a connoisseur of waters, bottled and still. She was no stranger to achievement. At Marienbad she had successfully vacated herself. She enjoyed its surpassing cuisine, ice-cold enemas, gratifying stools.

Like Gaucho, it was unforgivable of her to so passively fall from grace.

::

"There's nothing quite as real," Gaucho told *Enquiring Minds*, "as watching oneself age better than one had hoped, when it is unnecessary to age at all."

It was his last interview. As the embargo lifted Gaucho's circumvention was complete. He was as forgotten as only household names are, Eddie Cantor, the Kardashians who had not left behind so much as an infinitesimal tenor of themselves.

Yolo tried to reach Daughn. Padded Cell was a professional, wrap-around service, the kind operators who like disc jockeys revealed what she was about to hear, and afterwards, a run-down of what she just heard.

"Cuz?"

"He's starching the linens," the operator said.

"I wasn't myself," Yolo confessed. "I was in the manufacture of prophecies."

Her life had been a roulette of asylums. She recalled booking a one-way standing-room ticket to Tortola, excited by turbulence, unconscious of the self-reliance she had never used and hadn't much of. Through his Rolleiflex she watched Wallis spend all her winnings. Marienbad was not a place to leave up or down but to leave.

"Your work is done, Yolo." The operator upsold her woodenly, as if from a script. "Why wait?"

It was the policy of Tortola's news vehicles not to broadcast statistics like Yolo, attempted suicides, a black strap daiquiri with a cyanide chaser, a stomach pumping. Her instruction was to bury her at Mountain View, as close to the Black Dahlia as possible. But her body had been stronger than her will. Her only allusion as to why she wanted to quit the terrestrial paradise was written in Lancombe on a pewter service tray –

Every day is just like the one that receded (sic) it

Barbasol Meringue

1 B/3B/RF Liam Galliac gave his interns access to his e-mail account and password long before was a household name. He was anticipating his future fame so they could write it along the way, as it was happening. "Your life's work," he told them, "should not be my life."

The interns were unpaid sabermetricians. Numbers told stories – except for money, in this case. They were paid in proximity, in a back-and-forth of cryptic texts and auto-graphed swag.

When homage is paid it is not refundable. In Liam's first year with the A's he kept his hair up and tight on the sides and took his hazing in stride. He was the lesser parts of blockbuster trades, one of the players to be named later. He over-practiced his signature, over-signed, diluting its value. On the road, on and off waivers, Liam felt the urge to be on the phone or Skype or Reddit what he was in person. It was not always translatable: afternoons of fungoes, long toss, the dugout safe for dissent except for rubber masks of Commissioner Selig which were not for parody but for Halloween, only. (Also, a fineable offense.) Then: a smooth-operating farm system, role models who nevertheless dip Copenhagen, tackling streakers, memories of imitating Griffey. The friction from pounding the basepaths had made his calves hairless by age 13, a crucial year in which he taped back his pectorals and batted fifth.

His eyesight was so poor the infield shaded him to opposite field. His wife was not always in the bleachers. She was his light but a dim one, like a remnant of moon through cloud cover. He was away from her on road games for 81 nights of the year, on a charter plane that was a decommissioned airliner, an old Pan Am. He spent the roadstands window shopping in the Sky Mall, casually invalidating the sportswriters' second-guesses, inverting their clichés and clapping in the cabin during rough landings as if after a mildly satisfying rom-com. He decried the slow elimination of incidentals such as pretzels or roasted peanuts which didn't cost anything except the price of business. The flight attendants still referred to themselves as stewardesses.

A house of cards was still a house.

"I'm a bird," Victoria said to him, "There's nothing to pollenate here. I wonder who they're going to trade you to. As long as it's not Cincinnati."

There was always a day after the day Victoria never thought would arrive: there was two days after, a fifth and sixth, and after a period of time that did not feel like no time at all, she was healed, she was well and whole again.

"I'm being dealt to Toronto," Liam told her one night. "It's not personal."

"Of course it's personal."

"You're heartbroken, don't be. Everyone in baseball was an Athletic at some point."

"The Blue Jays." Victoria exhaled. "I told you I was a bird."

Toronto was not the future of flying, but the fear of. Saying goodbye to his teammates Liam copped to an affinity for the Coliseum, unrivalled in its splendor except for San Quentin, which Victoria found beautiful, perched right there on the water.

It wasn't personal and it wasn't a game. It was work. Liam didn't smile after homering and Victoria refrained from kudos.

"Why do you all pie each other after those those silly walkoffs? Is that real pie?"

It wasn't. It was shaving cream on paper plates. Liam loved it but he was looking forward to Toronto. Bay Area life was unsteadiness, girls primping in Michelob mirrors, spaniels at dog runs with their barks amputated, exercising their owners on retractable leashes. California was nothing like what it once was: still part of the first-world technically, but floundering. Citrus trees were for martini peels; gardens were compulsory. Las Vegas, they decided, was the perfect place for a layover.

::

"Spirit Air. Never again," Victoria said at McCarron Airport. "One-hundred-bucks for a carry-on. I don't mind being nickeled but I hate being dimed."

She was less relaxed by the falling water outside the Bellagio than by the rushing water of the Mirage. The Imperial Palace was equivalent to hospice. Liam did not play poker to win. Card sharps treated Vegas as a bank; others, a charity.

There was no other desert city. Casino war fascinated Victoria, as did six-leg parlays, the strippers who carpooled in from Henderson, the cloud patterns which like life's patterns were barometric tricks of the light. She wanted to dance in cages. She asked about the going rate for a lap dance.

"William Hung," she said. "I'm surprised he's not playing the Tropicana."

Conversation by pastiche. She was convinced that it wasn't his managing but numerology that helped Pete Rose gamble on the Reds. In her perch in the wooden Adirondacks at Jimmy Buffett's Margaritaville she was glad she wasn't like the other tourists, pacified by *La Reve* or day-long buffet access or helicopter tours of the Grand Canyon.

"I can't drink this," she said.

"Margaritas are your lifeblood. Taming yourself?"

Liam was in sunglasses, coke-bottles, so the tourists coursing by couldn't tell he was judging them. He saw Victoria through her whiskey and mescal phases, which were the same lenses through which he regulated himself. When she announced she was bored he suggested she play the ponies at the Gulfstream or Aqueduct, or the greyhounds in Sarasota who, the minute they stopped running in the money, were dumped into shallow ponds in the 'Glades.

"You see, they can't swim," Liam said.

Las Vegas. The psyche of shut-ins, deadbolts. The right place for the wrong people.

"Just because we're on vacation doesn't mean our troubles are behind us," she said. "You didn't have to get traded to Toronto. You didn't hustle. You didn't run."

"It's called a walk, not a run."

"You're supposed to hustle!"

Las Vegas. It was not stressful. Victoria took a breath and let the architecture affect her. Liam had wanted to check his blood pressure at Walgreens, but an old lady was sitting in the chair, arm-deep in the compressed cuff, eating ice cream.

"Harrah's smells like defeat and Virginia Slims. Ah, it's exhausting, I'm exhausting," she said. "Your road women. When you're on the road."

Liam admitted nothing, denied everything. Demanded proof.

"We spoke in New York," she said. "You told me all

about it."

"Give me a play-by-play."

"Your message was truncated, as usual."

"I'm sure it was only a lavatory tryst," he said. "A party kiss."

"In New York," she said, "against the Yankees, you were grinding to Neil Young."

"Not during the game."

"You browned out in Greenwich Village."

"Did I slur?"

"You never slur."

"As long as I didn't slur," Liam said.

"You called from a pay phone."

"Do they still make those?"

A city of razed hotels, The Riviera, the Sahara, obsolete like those team mascots who once were Redskins, Arabs. Victoria lounged back, obtusely sitting. Margaritaville was apt. It was a progressive marriage, not a fucked-up marriage.

"She didn't mean anything," Liam said. "Whoever this girl was."

"That makes it worse. You kissed her and then you said you did the hardy-har. What the hell is the hardy-har? Is that like the Macarena?"

"I'm retiring," Liam said. "I'm retiring today from women."

It was supposed to relax her: a pedicure and four hours by the pool. Blackjack.

"You said you were proud of me," Liam said.

"When?"

"You accused me of being clutch this year, of being a spark plug."

"Stop," she said. "Quit while we're tied. Remember how competitive I was in high school? Where'd that go?"

"I remember," Liam said. He was huge in the Adirondack; his forearm was wider than the arm rest. "You beat me in the finals."

"You blubbered."

"I was a blubberer. You argued me clear across the room."

"To think you gave up debate for baseball," she said.

An hour and five margaritas had passed. They were Marilyn Monroe and Joe DiMaggio, incarnate. Liam loved Victoria. In her own way, she absolutely despised him.

"I could sit here all day," she said.

"Look, let's forget all of this," Liam said. "Smoke out later?"

"Marijuana? Where?"

"In our suite, where else?"

"There's a recovery fee," Victoria said.

"We can afford it."

"But what are we're going to do about the IRS? They want $63,000."

Liam kissed his biceps.

"Tell them to put it on my tab," he said.

Toronto never materialized. It's sad to hear Liam these days, announcing games on KNBR: he hasn't the voice for it, or the old quickness, or the heart. His number is retired nowhere. As for Victoria … the fog will always burn off. She doesn't have to pray for it.

Q & A's

A SHORT PLAY

–　You're not nervous?

—　Not nervous but at the precipice of it.

–　You got yourself a roll of gaffers' tape, good.

—　I'm blocking.

–　Stage right is on your left. Think of what the audience sees.

—　It's clear I don't know what I'm doing.

–　I don't think it's that clear. Pass over those headshots.

—　Slim pickings. There's a problem with this guy in particular.

–　Crispus Attucks.

—　That's some stage name.

–　He survived Tisch.

—　He won't do. It's too dark.

–　That's just the toner. Do me a solid, try him out.

—　We should have asked for color photos.

–　You put out a casting call for an August Wilson play and expect white applicants?

—　Naïve, yes. I'll cop to that.

–　Don't you ever wonder?

—　No.

–　I think we'll be run out of town.

—　No.

–　Tarred and feathered.

—　It won't be that bad.

– Assistant, — Producer, ⋯ Crispus (actor)

– We'll be Molotoved. It's a good thing your building has a doorman.

– This has to be done. Help me block.

– You've got the shoe-shine set up on stage left?

– The script didn't come with instructions. It's not a microwave dinner.

– It's not a script. It's a play. This isn't Warner Bros. This isn't Moneyball.

– Look, I saw *Sunday in the Park*.

– On VHS.

– I read Sondheim.

– You're making a play, not a hat.

– I read Lindsay-Abaire.

– You're ranting.

– I haven't started. Forgive the pun, but put yourself in my shoes. Your old man, a scumlord, kicks the bucket in Seattle and he leaves you the property and all the renters.

– What a windfall.

– You've read James Purdy, Dos Passos.

– Your shoes are showing.

– You've read Kazan and Miller. The end of *Waiting for Lefty* gives you that tingling sensation up your leg.

– The you in this story is definitely not me.

– At the cross-section of your new money and wanderlust and being orphaned you find lodging in Capital Hill above Venus Bar which they have razed and while razing it …

- I drank there once. It was like getting drunk in a portable toilet.
- But before they've demolished it you find …
- *You* find.
- This manuscript, in the insulation.
- You didn't know who August Wilson was.
- No. I'm a Black man from the suburbs. We were the Cosbys.
- You don't know Wendy Wasserstein. You've never seen *Rent*. It could be anyone's.
- But Wilson slept in pops' building, he *rented*, for four months in 1972.
- It could have been your pops' manuscript. Any nut with a typewriter.
- Christie's said it could be Wilson's. His estate said it was in his, what's the word, *idiolect*.
- A one-act about a black shoe-shine who sees auras, set in California and played by a white actor? No wonder you took up smoking. How do those work, by the way?
- Batteries. You can't extinguish electronic smokes. That's part of the joy.
- Too bad Wilson's not around to ask. Have you thought?
- Yes. Extensively.
- Have you thought that he could be wrong? About the casting. It won't fly. You're shooting for moons.
- Remember freshman year when you put on *Death of a Salesman*?
- A spineless text. Everyone does it.

— Are you allowed to change anything?

— We took small liberties. We did it in the nude.

— But you can't change the dialogue.

— No.

— Not even to modernize it.

— I see your point but I don't see your right.

— Wilson wanted a certain type of actor.

— Says Wilson?

— Right here in the margin notes.

— Says Wilson's scumlord.

— Look, I didn't find this script. It found me.

— I can't see how you think this is OK.

— A Black writer stipulates he doesn't want Black actors for his work.

— It makes me uncomfortable. I feel like I felt when we traded away Grant Green.

— If Wilson were white ...

— If he was white there'd be no *Fences*, no *Radio Golf.* It doesn't sit right. You think race has nothing to do with it.

— I think *color* has nothing to do with it.

— It's good you're financing this yourself. I'm not sure if anyone else would. Maybe Bob Jones University. I'm like the best man here, I'm supposed to remind you the night before that you don't have to go through with it, we can fly to Mexico, and right now all you've sunk into this is a deposit for the black box and ... gaffer's tape.

— Notice what people wear backstage?

–   We stage managers, yes.

–   You wear black.

–   Yes.

–   To blend in.

–   It's our home uniform. It's also a slimming color.

–   Do you know of any good ones?

–   Don't ask me to. I'm a lowly ASM. I'm sort of like that backup catcher we see in the bullpen: the A does not stand for Ambition.

–   You're not seeking fame.

–   Not infamy, no. That play belongs in a museum, not onstage. You don't know theatre. It's warfare. It's receipts. Cussing out your actors. It's the Marines.

···   Hello? Is this Oakland Repertory? Door was unlocked.

–   It's the wrong neighborhood for it.

···   I'm not used to driving around Temescal. Crispus Attucks. I have a 12:15.

–   Thanks for coming on such notice. Get settled, give us your vitals.

···   5′9″," 150. I was in *Tempestuousness*, directed by Sam Gold at the Duke.

–   I know Sam. We got drunk in a toy teepee once. He cuts his pot with loose tobacco.

–   Go on.

···   That was after Tisch …

— Tisch?

… That's NYU.

— What's the part?

— You're Sway. Your name is Sway. You're a shoe-shine.

… Where?

— Here, Oakland. Outside the old Kaiser building. You see auras. You're black.

… Am I miming it?

— You'll have polish and a towel.

… No, what you said about the black. As in, black sheep?

— As in, minstrel.

— We'd like for you to read a side for us.

… A cold read?

— Starting at the top of 5.

… Where's page 6?

— Before you start remove the hat.

… You have something against the A's?

— No, but hat's off.

— I don't know. Wouldn't a shoe-shine wear the hometeam cap?

… I do everything in this hat. It's my hat.

— It's not in the script.

— Play.

… Forgive me, but you sound like one of those.

 – One of what?

   ⋯ I can't say.

 – Humor him.

   ⋯ You know, a *Giants* fan.

 – He's partial to the Mariners.

    ⋯ Is it alright if I call you Frisco?

 – Crispus doesn't seem to want the part.

   ⋯ Some housekeeping first. This is
    August Wilson.

 – Correct.

   ⋯ Well, how do you know?

 – I found it. Right there, his signature affirms it.

   ⋯ But why now? It's not exactly
    calm, if you know what I mean.
    Societally.

 – Explain it to Crispus.

 – For starters, a Black man in America has to work twice
  as hard.

   ⋯ I'm not disagreeing.

 – And shoeshines were everywhere, before the suede fad.

 – Have you ever done anything, Crispus, that you find
  morally reprehensible?

   ⋯ Yes. I was in *South Pacific*.

 – So have I. I was Vince Fontaine once, from *Grease*, and
  they wouldn't let me sing. But I know how to make
  cameos. I read history. I like to see things finished. I like
  fruition.

··· But is it worthwhile to produce an artist's every lark? I mean, would you produce a one-act of the phone numbers he wrote on cocktail napkins, or a dramatic reading of his tax returns?

— It doesn't read like a lark. It's about identity. We carry confirmations of us around on little laminate cards, not for ourselves, but to prove who we are. Race could be creed, gender … they're all euphemisms for the same thing.

— The play is also about fidelity.

— And frontiers. Men are breastfeeding. Clothes malfunction on TV. It's about exploiting sensitivities.

··· Even one audition these days is a windfall. Can't look a gift horse. Tell me about Sway.

— Sway smells roses. Literally. In the street he stops.

··· Here in Oakland?

— He's guessing. It doesn't really say.

··· Homeboy really liked Pittsburg, I know that.

— This isn't *Jitney*. He shines shoes. He's not negotiating cab fares. Page 5, at the top. Go.

— *Black man wiping shoes, no surprise. Black man golfing, running for mayor, now that's money. It like Wilt when he made 100. If you on fire in life you don't feel the flame. Can't see them but dey there. Dey here.*

— This is where you take a shine.

- If he's equity, that'll cost extra.
- What's equity?
- The union. If he uses props he gets hazard pay.

> ··· *Had me work once, money. A woman. She tall. Had to be this high to ride her. But the fine print was in disappearing ink. She say, chores, do dem. I spend enough time on my knees, I say. She put forty pounds on me and she say she only meant for twenty of it. She want out. She think she the great white hope. You ain't great, I say, and you isn't white and you is sure as hell ain't hope. When you land yourself in the dunk tank, I say, I hope there are sharks.*

- Are you equity?

> ··· Naturally. Wouldn't I also have an apron in this scene?

- No. Shoe polish. It would rub off.
- As you shined.

> ··· And by the end I'd …

- Grow into my color.
- Turn your color.

> ··· Ah-ha.

- See, it has to be Wilson's. No white man could think that up. Keep reading.

> ··· *You get older, the hills get steeper. You not out of breath. But you breathing.*

- This is where you pull out your piece.

           ··· Is that necessary?

– There's always a gun in August Wilson. It doesn't always go off.

           ··· Yes it do, Frisco.

– Not in *Jitney*.

– Call him narcissism, but don't call him Frisco.

           ··· A gun onstage always go off.

– Wait, are you still in character? No gunfire. It's just cocked.

           ··· You cocked. *Being boss is easy. Boss don't work. Boss sit all day. Boss meet all day. So I say to him, the way you pay a man, he go three Fridays without money. That's three weekends he's watching his wallet. Who told you that make sense? Man work an hour he get paid that hour. Man shine a shoe he get paid for that shoe.*

– You're in character.

           ··· *You don't know how good you got it, boss say. You right, I say. Last November when I got that pox, how good I have it then. I gave you a day off, he say. Unpaid, I say. A Friday, he say. You had the whole weekend, he say.*

– Let him stay in character.

           ··· *White man give a Black man a weekend, he think it a gift. He think he Santa Claus.*

– Stay in.